THE BETRAYED

A PECOS QUINN WESTERN – BOOK 1

JOHN ROSE PUTNAM

The Betrayed
(A Pecos Quinn Western – Book 1)

Paperback Edition
Copyright © 2018 by John Rose Putnam

Wolfpack Publishing
6032 Wheat Penny Avenue
Las Vegas, NV 89122

All rights reserved. No part of this book may be reproduced by any means without the prior written consent of the publisher, excepting brief quotes used in reviews.

Paperback ISBN: 978-1-64119-445-7
ebook ISBN: 978-1-64119-444-0

Library of Congress Control Number: 2018961086

THE BETRAYED

1

"You looking for Mr. Brantley, Mister?" the boy asked, his head hung low so the fierce sun would stay above the frayed straw brim of his old, beat up sombrero.

He sat nearly hidden in a tiny speck of shade from a rocky outcrop beside the trail. Maybe thirteen he was covered from head to toe by the dust that obscured everything in this desolate place. Even the mesquite and gray, green sagebrush along this rolling prairie was coated with it.

I took off my once proud hat and wiped my forehead. It too was caked with a brown plaque that had turned it into a road-weary, formless, shapeless, pate covering sunscreen that sported a darker stripe where the constant sweat from my brow had soaked through.

"What if I am?" I replied.

He looked up for the first time and quickly shaded

his eyes with the flat palm of a sunburned hand. "If ya are I reckon I'm supposed to tell Mr. Brantley."

I pointed to the town nearly a mile away, the few buildings shimmering in waves from the torrid, overheated air. "Are you going to run over there in this heat?"

"Oh, Mr. Brantley ain't in town. He's out at the ranch."

"I see, so you tell Brantley whenever a stranger comes to town. Is he your pa?"

"Well, yes sir and no sir. I tell him about strangers but he ain't my pa."

Somehow hearing Brantley wasn't the boy's pa was welcome news. Whatever might happen here would be easier if I knew the boy wouldn't be an orphan. "The ranch must be pretty far from here?" I asked, hoping for more information about the boss.

"It sure is." He perked up. "I got a horse behind the rocks. There's a spring, some shade and a little grass. I ride Willow out to the spread. She's old but she likes me. I like her too."

He smiled real wide when he talked about his horse. His blue eyes sparkled while sandy hair dangled out from under the straw of his hat. He reminded me of someone, a boy from a long time ago, before the war. Everything from before the war seemed so terribly long ago.

"What're you doing with all that artillery, Mister?" he asked and his honest observation yanked me back to the here and now.

"Oh, you mean the pistols?"

"Most folks are lucky to have one. Mr. Brantley is the only guy I know to have as many as you got and yours dangle out all over, one on each side and one under your arm."

"A six-shooter won't do you much good if you can't get to it fast, son."

"Did you shoot a lot of folks with them?" he asked and I could hear his eagerness.

"I fought Comanche in Texas, but killing folks, even Indians, isn't such a good thing."

"Comanche, holy cow, they're right fierce I hear tell."

I didn't answer, not because I had nothing to say but because I didn't want to remember. There had been too much killing, first Comanche, next the war, then Comanche again. I had to wonder, since it looked like I'd found Brantley, would it come to an end at last?

"I've been riding a long time in the hot sun," I told him. "How about you share some of that cool spring water and shade with my horse and me? We'd both be mighty grateful?"

He looked up again, a worried expression on his face. "Mr. Brantley will have my hide if I don't tell him you're here."

"Oh, is he all that interested in strangers who come to town?"

"There's been some who tried to do him hurt. I reckon it's something about the war."

The boy had hit the nail on the head. This was the

Brantley I was looking for. "I guess he has a lot of riders on his ranch. Those riders would be gun hands I'd bet, mostly ex-soldiers."

"He says they're just cowhands but a lot have their pistols slung low like you do. I reckon there's a couple a dozen. I can't say any of them wear more than one or two guns though."

"I suppose he'll send a few men out to talk to me after you tell him I'm here."

"Yeah, maybe three or four, there's been trouble with saddle tramps lately."

"Is that what I am, a saddle tramp?"

"I reckon so, but you're about the friendliest one I seen in a while."

"Does that mean I'm friendly enough to share some shade and cool water with?"

He gave me a wide boyish grin and hopped to his feet. "Sure you are. Come on," he said as he waved me on. I followed him up a narrow path around the rock outcrop where a tiny stream flowed out from a spring that bubbled up from beneath a rock overhang. The boy's horse stood under the shade of that overhang nibbling at the grass there. A small cottonwood tree grew beside the water and a swath of thick green grass continued along the stream for quite a way.

I grabbed my two canteens and dropped down to the creek, leaving the sorrel to take his fill beside me. Then I took off my hat and dumped handfuls of the cool water over my head before I drank what I needed.

I filled both canteens and looped them over the saddle horn.

At first the boy followed me with his eyes while he patted the neck of his mare. Now he seemed nervous and his gaze moved off in the distance along the route the stream followed. I turned to see a large dust cloud billowing up. Riders were coming this way.

"I need to go Mister," he said. "Those are Brantley's men. They come by here every day to check on me. If they find you and me here together I'll get a whooping. I don't want that."

"I see. Brantley doesn't like strangers much, does he?"

"No sir, he don't like anybody as far as I can tell."

"What'll happen if I ride into town?"

"They'll come after you. Then, if you give them cause, they'll kill you."

I swung into the saddle. "How many riders are coming?" I asked him.

"I don't know for sure, three or four usually."

"You go and meet them. Tell them I'm looking for work. I'll be on my way now."

"Thanks Mister."

"Thank you, son, the water and shade were most welcome. What's your name?"

"Andy, sir."

"Andy, that's a great name." I tugged at my hat brim and rode back around the rock. The boy's name hit me hard. I'd had a son once. Was his name Andy too? It seemed like it was, but that was before the war and things from back then had been lost somewhere, somehow.

Just outside of town I saw the sign. It was nothing but a sun bleached board nailed to a stake. The whole thing leaned to the left and seemed ready to fall over. It said Brantleyville, population 100 in faded black paint. The number had been crossed through and someone had scribbled 87 below it. I wondered if that number included Brantley's ranch.

The town itself wasn't anything to crow about, but how it could be stuck out here in the middle of nowhere was beyond me. Tumble weeds blew across the only street. There were three buildings. I headed for the Brantley Saloon opposite a desolate looking hotel.

The bat wing doors creaked loud when I walked in. I wondered if that was from lack of use. Only two people were inside. A dark haired fellow in clothes as ragged as what Andy wore sat at a table by the window nursing a half empty glass and didn't look up. A scrawny barkeep in a starched white shirt and sporting a black, waxed mustache and goatee stood behind a highly polished mahogany bar hard at work wiping clean glasses with a dirty rag. His face floated in and out of the fog of the past. Did I know him from somewhere? I had no answer.

"What'll it be," he asked without looking up.

"A cold beer would be a Godsend," I said.

"No beer, Mister, too far from anywhere for beer,

and there ain't never been nothing cold here. We got whiskey and liquor. Take your pick."

"What's the difference?"

"Whiskey's cheaper, liquor's better."

"I'll have the liquor."

"Good choice." He poured a shot into one of the glasses he'd just wiped and slid it down the bar. It stopped in front of me without spilling a drop.

"That's quite an arsenal you're wearing. What brings you to Brantleyville?" he went on.

"I heard a fellow here was looking for gun hands."

"Are you any good with those Colts?"

"The Comanche thought so." I dropped a coin on the bar and sat at a nearby table.

"You in the late war?" he asked as he went back to wiping his glassware.

"Anybody here really care?" I said and then took a sip of the liquor. It was bad. Next time I'd try the whiskey, if there was a next time.

"Something seems familiar about you. You know Colonel Brantley?" he asked.

I took another sip of the booze. "I was in the war, but I don't remember much about it."

Several riders reined in outside. One yelled, "That must be his horse. He's inside."

Boots clomped across the wooden walkway. The bat wing doors creaked loud and three men strode into the saloon. Two wore big Colts slung low. The other had a two gun rig strapped on. That made it even, I thought. They had four guns. I had four guns.

"Whiskey all around, Pete," Two Guns called as they headed straight to the bar.

Pete plopped a jug down with three of his freshly polished glasses. They all had a quick shot. Then Two Guns turned to me. I wondered why it took him so long.

"You're a stranger here, ain't ya Mister?"

"I'm not a stranger anywhere. I've known myself my whole life."

He roared with laughter. "Is that what your Mama taught ya, smartass? It's real cute."

"She was a wonderful woman," I told him, my right hand wrapped tight around my glass.

Then, without even blinking, he went for the hogleg on his right hip. Before he'd cleared leather I had my short barreled hideout gun cocked and pointed at his gut. "Take your hand away from that pistol real slow, big boy, or you'll have a brand new bellybutton right quick, courtesy of my mother's only full grown son."

"Oh, you got me wrong, stranger. I wasn't going for my gun," he whined. His hands were showing now, palms toward me and a foot or so above the pearl handles on his matched set of Navy Colts. His two companions leaned against the bar, looking at their compadre with wide grins, likely enjoying his comeuppance, and sucking up whiskey as fast as they could.

"Oh. I know you weren't going to draw on me. You just wanted to scratch your rear, isn't that right big boy? What's the name you're going by these days?"

He spit a black mouthful from his chaw onto the floor by my boot. "They call me Ringo."

"You'd best be careful, Ringo. You don't have nine lives like a cat."

"You got the drop on me now, but things can change real fast."

"Get on your horse, Ringo. Ride back to where you came from and let Colonel Brantley know Pecos Quinn is waiting here for him. Tell him to come alone. Take these two whiskey guzzlers with you. If I see any of you again I just might kill you."

"Mr. Brantley, he ain't going to like this."

"Do as you're told, Ringo, and we'll get along fine."

"We ain't ever going to get along, Mister."

"You'll be in better shape if you hurry up and get out of here," I suggested real calm like.

He started backing away toward the door. I let go my liquor glass and pulled a second Colt with my right hand, cocked it and waved it at the two whiskey guzzlers. They started for the open air outside too. The hinges on the saloon doors groaned loud as all three men left. I heard their horses riding off and went to the door to check. Then I spun back to the bar and leveled my Colt at the barkeep. "Put that scattergun down, Pete, right now."

He started to shake but he put the gun down.

"Now walk over to the end of the bar near where I was sitting and keep your hands up so I can see them. You and me can have a friendly conversation, just like we're old pals."

He did as he was told. I grabbed my drink as I passed the table and staked out a spot at the end of the bar just around the corner from where he stood. Here I could see anyone riding up the road through the window or catch them as they walked in the door. I could also keep up with the barkeep too. It might be a while before Brantley showed up.

The man by the window was still sitting there. He hadn't moved. It was like he could care less what happened inside the saloon. "What's with our friend, Pete?" I wondered.

"Better you don't know," he answered.

"It can't be worse than the war."

"It was after the war. The Comanche got his wife and daughter. He's been that way ever since. The Colonel brought him back here. He just sits and drinks, never talks much at all."

I downed my shot. He filled the glass from the same jug the three gunmen left behind. "This one's on your friends," he said. "Ringo has a point. He'll have to kill you now. You showed him up. He doesn't like that."

"Ringo is already dead, just like the fellow by the door. He looks familiar too, like you do. He was in the war wasn't he? So were you?"

"Pete Conroy, Pecos. Like you I served with Colonel Brantley."

"And him?" I pointed to the guy by the door.

"Paine Dodd, at least that's what we call him, but he never answers."

"That name rings a bell. He had a ranch near mine."

Pete's eyebrows rose. He leaned in close. "You don't remember the war do you?"

"Bits and pieces, I remember the Comanche."

"The war was over. We were all trying to make it home before the Yankees caught us when we got jumped by the Comanche. You got hit. We thought you were dead."

I shook my head. I didn't remember a thing. "You left me behind, didn't you?"

"We had no choice. Half of us got away. The rest didn't. That's the breaks."

"Paine Dodd got away."

"The Comanche had just been to his ranch. That's where we been before they jumped us. Dodd broke when he saw what happened there. He ain't been the same since."

I didn't ask what happened. I'd seen it too many times at too many homesteads. "I saw the sign outside town," I muttered. "It said a hundred people live here. Somebody scratched that out and wrote in eighty-seven below it. That's not much of a town, is it?"

"Maybe you weren't looking close, Pecos. It ain't much of a town."

"Who died, Pete?"

He took in a deep breath and looked out the window to the road I came in on. I wondered if he hoped to see Colonel Brantley heading this way and maybe he could stall long enough that he wouldn't have to answer my question. Then I wondered why it was I thought he didn't want to answer me. Why did I have a lingering feeling that something was terribly wrong here?

"I don't know how that sign got there. I don't even know if there were ever a hundred folks living here. About the only people who live in town are the ones like Dodd. There's maybe a dozen over at the hotel. Dodd's in the best shape of all of them. The Colonel takes care of the whole lot. He built this town just to give them a sense they belong somewhere. He pays for their food and even their liquor, those still in good enough shape to drink anyhow."

"You mean to tell me this is a town built to hold a dozen men broken when the Comanche raided their spreads at the end of the war?"

"Men and women but that's pretty much it. Oh, the hands at the ranch come to town for a drink now and then. Brantley pays for that too, but other than that nothing ever happens here."

I stared at the barkeep. The lost wheels in my mind spinning, the ones I still had contact with whispering to me that what Pete said was a lie, a total bald-faced fabrication so farfetched that I couldn't accept that anyone would believe it.

Yet I had seen the Comanche. I'd been to the places they raided. What they left behind would break even the strongest man. That's what the Comanche wanted to do, crush the will of the white eyes so we would leave the land they claimed as theirs. We were beating them back, insuring the safety of our families and our ranches when the war came. The enemy suddenly changed from Indians to Yankees and we all went off to fight our new foe.

But another part of my mind cried out that Pete told the truth. I'd been having the same dream night after night. It drove me out here to this desolate wilderness. My own spread, right next to Dodd's, had been raided by Indians. Everyone I loved was gone, but when I woke up the dream would soon fade into the black depths of liquor, until I finally put the whiskey down and went after the truth. But the memories were still locked behind a curtain of pain, the dream masked by the unreality of the end. I'd been shot in that dream. I woke up thinking I was dead.

"Are you all right, Pecos? You're talking to yourself," Pete said sounding concerned.

"I need to talk to Dodd," I told him and walked over to the scattergun on the bar and picked it up. "I'll keep this close, just in case any Comanche show up."

"That's funny, Pecos, but they ain't around here anymore."

"I reckon not the redskin kind anyhow, but you never know."

I sat down by Dodd. He didn't look at me. I wasn't even sure he knew I was there. "It's been a long time, Paine. How are you? It's me, Pecos Quinn, or Paul Quinn back in better days."

He turned his head slowly to me, his eyes cloudy, lost in the whiskey. "They killed my Lorena and my pretty Maryann. They were my whole world, Paul. Oh God the things they did."

"I know how ruthless—"

"Shush," he said in a soft and all too sane whisper, perhaps so the barkeep wouldn't hear. "I don't want to talk about Comanche. Leave me alone. I got nothing left. They took everything I had. My whole life was gone in a flash of white man's gunpowder. They did it to you too, Paul Quinn, but somehow you came back for more. Run Paul, save yourself while you can. Take the boy with you. He doesn't deserve what Carter Brantley will do to him. Run for your lives."

Then he leaped to his feet, hate fully over his unshaven face, and threw the chair he'd sat in across the room. "Leave me be, Pecos Quinn," he screamed. "I saw all I care to see of the Comanche. They killed my wife and daughter. That's enough, more than enough." He grabbed the whiskey jug. The doors screamed as he stormed out into the heat of the sun.

I sat back in the chair, stunned at what just happened. Paine Dodd seemed like two different men, one totally lucid, warning me of coming trouble, the other a raving madman who threw a chair like a lunatic. Did the Comanche do this to him? Or was it someone else?

He whispered to me that I should save myself. Then he urged me to take the boy with me. What was it about the boy that ate at my insides so? Maybe he reminded me of myself when I was young. Still, I had to know what happened to me, and yes, to Paine Dodd as well as the boy.

"That's the way they are, Pecos." Pete said. "Sometimes they can be friendly as a new puppy and others they're as mean as an overheated rattler."

I looked back to the bar. Pete hadn't moved. He didn't seem worried by Paine Dodd's outburst. Maybe it was now normal but I remembered him as a good neighbor and friend. We'd helped each other with round-ups and either planting or harvesting our small crops. We shared Sunday suppers often with his family. My kid played with his, at least until the war came. Paine and I were together in almost every fight, all the way up to the end. And then that last fracas wasn't with the Yankees, it was with the Comanche again. Or was it? Something didn't add up.

I went to the swinging doors and looked out over the top. Paine Dodd crossed the street and walked into the hotel. No one else was around. This had to be the loneliest town I'd ever seen. The people who lived here must stay inside. In this heat I didn't blame them.

With the shotgun still in my hand I headed back to the bar. Pete had stayed where he was. He seemed in no hurry to escape my clutches if I actually even had him in them. After all this was his bar and he must feel perfectly at home here.

Then it hit me. I hadn't seen a single horse on the street. I didn't recall seeing a stable or even a blacksmith shop on my way in. I would bet that no stage stopped here. The residents, like Paine Dodd and the others in the Brantley Hotel, were trapped, prisoners in a jail without walls.

I looked hard at Pete as I returned to the bar. "Dodd

must stay at the hotel. Where do you live, Pete?" I asked him, hoping it sounded like just another casual question.

"I got a room in the back," he said as he took a swipe over the top of his bar with the same rag he used to polish the glasses.

"Where do you keep your horse?"

"Oh, I don't need a horse. I never go anywhere except out to the ranch maybe once a month to talk to Colonel Brantley. Spend all my time here. We still have nine or ten good citizens who come in every day. Some get highly agitated if they don't get their whiskey."

The rag went back and forth, always over the same spot on the bar like it didn't matter if he ever did the whole thing only that he kept going through the motions. If Dodd was loco, could it be that Pete was too. Maybe everyone else in this two bit town was as far off their feed as these two were? Christ, I thought, maybe I belonged here with them.

I shook my head. Maybe I was as crazy as a loon, but I didn't want to stay in this one horse town and swill whiskey in Pete's bar with the likes of Dodd, as clearly crazy as he is now, and anyone else who lives in that hotel across the street. Somehow, slipping underneath that fog in my mind, I realized that Brantley would try to take my horse if he intended to keep me.

"Stay right where you are, Pete. I need a little more company while I wait." With that I headed back through the squeaky bar doors, untied the sorrel and walked him up the steps and across the boardwalk. He balked a bit at the bat wing doors but, with a few reassuring strokes on his neck, he followed me in. I tied him to the bar. Meanwhile Pete still wiped the same spot on the bar over and over again with his dirty rag, but he stared at the sorrel as if he were the devil himself.

"Do you have any food in this place, Pete?" I asked, and judging by how skinny he was I'd bet he almost never ate.

"Got some pickled cucumbers and boiled eggs. You want some?"

"Bring them on," I urged.

He walked halfway down the bar and grabbed two large jars. He pulled a pickle out of one and handed it to me.

"You go ahead, Pete. Take a bite."

"Sure," he said, "don't mind if I do." He took a big chomp out of it.

I felt better but pushed the eggs closer to him. "Now have one of these."

Again he helped himself this time with a smile. I followed his lead and had a half dozen boiled eggs and as many pickled cucumbers. "These are good, Pete."

"Mrs. Mallory at the Brantley Diner brings a fresh batch every day. She'll be by later."

The name sounded familiar. The slow wagon wheels inside my head started rolling again. Dodd's ranch was south of mine, Blake Mallory's north. "Is her name Esther, Pete?"

"Damn if it ain't," he muttered as he fished in the jar for more eggs.

I heard horses coming up the road from where I'd met the boy long before I saw them. I pulled the Henry rifle from a scabbard on the sorrel and walked to the side window, still holding the scattergun in my left hand mostly to keep it away from Pete. Six men were coming, one, decked out in a wide brimmed straw Panama planters' hat and sitting high atop a proud Morgan adorned with a fancy Mexican silver studded saddle, had to be Carter Brantley.

I let them get closer then braced the scattergun against the wall and cocked the lever of the Henry. "Good to see you, Carter," I yelled. "Leave your riders outside and come in alone."

"That you, Pecos? It's been as long time. These are all men who rode with us in the war. They were your friends then. It'll be good to get together again."

"We can have a party later, Carter. Right now you and me need to talk one on one."

"I have a lot of enemies left over from the war. These men are my bodyguards. They stay with me," he hollered back.

I fired a shot at the foot of the lead rider's horse. The paint reared high on his hind legs. Meanwhile I jacked another cartridge into the chamber and did the same thing to the next horse and the one after that until all five horses were bucking and out of control.

Brantley sat calm in his silver encrusted saddle, his horse unfazed. He finally called out. "I get your point,

Pecos. You were always one hell of a marksman. My men will stay out here where you can see them. I'll come in alone."

"Leave the hog-leg outside," I yelled.

He took off the pistol belt and hooked it over his saddle horn. While he rode to the front of the saloon I walked over to the swinging doors and watched him tie the Morgan to the rail and head this way, unarmed.

I backed up against the front wall and waited for Brantley to come in. Soon the doors screamed again and a big, distinguished looking man with white hair and side whiskers strode in.

After several steps he turned around. "How are you, Pecos? It's been a few years. This comes as a surprise. I thought you were dead."

"Seems like I might have been. Sometimes I wonder myself."

"The boy told Ringo you were looking for work."

"Depends on what kind of work you got, Colonel."

"That was damn good shooting with the Henry."

"I told Ringo that you needed to come alone."

"I don't take orders from Ringo. He takes them from me."

"Was he in the war?"

"He made sergeant in third troop right before the fighting ended."

"Now he's your second in command?"

"He runs things for me."

"He doesn't look like a cow hand."

"No, Ringo doesn't work cows. I have other men for that."

"Ringo does your killing then."

"Pecos, what happened to you? We rode together for four years. We fought together. You led the first troop. The men in it would follow you anywhere. You were smart, brave and had the heart of a lion. I depended on you. I don't know how many times you saved us all."

"What did happen to me, Brantley?"

"That's a hard subject. Why don't we sit down? Pete, bring us some of my brandy."

I pointed to the table near my sorrel. "We'll sit over there. My horse gets lonely."

"We don't usually allow animals in town, Pecos, much less in the bar."

"I noticed how lonesome it looked here."

We sat. Pete brought a fine French brandy and filled two glasses.

"The war was over," Brantley began. "We were running from Yankee cavalry. Not a man among us wanted to surrender to them. We got to Dodd's spread. The Comanche had just been there. It was worse than anything I ever saw in the war. Dodd lost his mind. He hasn't been the same since. You rode off to your place alone, and must have come across Comanche. When we got there you looked stone dead. Then the Yankees attacked. We had to ride fast."

"Clearly I wasn't dead, Brantley. You left me to die."

"You would have done the same thing to me if I'd

been flat on the ground with blood pouring out of my head and chest and the Yankee horse soldiers bearing down on you."

"Would I?" The edge in my voice rang out clear. "At least I would have checked you close enough to know for sure. The Thirty-ninth Texas didn't leave men behind."

"The Thirty-ninth Texas was on the run. The Yankees won the damn war. We didn't surrender and hand over our weapons like we were ordered. That was a crime. We were outlaws. Their horse soldiers were told to shoot us on sight, and we both know they relished that idea."

"Then why didn't they shoot me?"

"How the hell do I know? Maybe they thought you were dead too." He drained his brandy glass. Pete was at his side in a heartbeat to fill it.

An image filled my mind's eye. Colonel Carter Brantley dined alone at a table outside his tent before the battle of Shiloh somewhere in Tennessee. He feasted on a young roast pullet served on fine china and washed down with French Champagne from a crystal wine glass that had been constantly topped off by his loyal aide, Corporal Peter Conroy. Meanwhile the rest of the troopers, myself included, supped on cornbread and beans and not enough of that.

"Maybe they weren't there?" I shot back.

He put the brandy glass down. "How can you say that, Pecos? You were with us the whole time. You knew they were close on our tail. Somebody must have saved your life but it sure wasn't the Yankees. Do you remember anything?"

"I remember old Molly McCall. She must have been ninety when I woke up in her cabin. She'd cared for me for a few weeks, always thinking I'd die before the next sun rose. I'm still not sure if I disappointed her or not, but I'll forever thank her for what she did. We never had a chance to talk about how I got there. She passed on before I was near ready to fend for myself. I managed to survive the next few days before some squatters found me. They kept Molly's cabin and gave me the boot when I was well enough to travel. I've been putting the pieces together ever since. Someday they'll fall into place, maybe sooner than later. Those memories led me here."

Anger flashed across his face like a hot fire over a field of dry grass. Why would the possibility of me finding out the lost memories of my life irritate Carter Brantley?

I locked onto his black eyes and held his angry glare in check. I had more to say. "Whoever found me loaded my near dead carcass onto a wagon and carted me to Mrs. McCall's place, near a day away. They likely weren't worried about Comanche or Yankee. Who do you think would do a thing like that, and right after you and your troops had fled like scared rabbits from the same Union Cavalry we'd whipped time after time all the way across Texas?"

"Don't you dare call my troops cowards, you rotten deserter."

"I'm afraid you are the one who said your troops abandoned their fallen officer in the field of battle and fled the onslaught of the Yankee horse soldiers, Colonel, not me."

"Damn you, Quinn. I'll not entertain talk like that from any man."

"I'm not any man, Brantley. I'm the wounded man you abandoned on the battlefield."

"We had to go, damn it. They outnumbered us ten to one."

"And so you fled in the same direction the Comanche had gone."

"The Comanche went west. We rode north."

"That day someone burned every homestead north of my place for ten miles."

"We had to flank them while they were busy. You know I always have scouts out."

"And if the Yankee bowlegs were behind you they would have run into the Comanche."

"Damn you, Quinn. I told you what happened. We skirted the Comanche and outran the Union horse. After we got out of Texas they left us alone. By then most of us had gone home. We had only a handful of men when we got here. You can think what you want."

He swilled down the brandy in his glass. Pete refilled it at once. I wondered how Brantley managed to drink at home when he didn't have his trusted aide around to keep the booze flowing. Maybe he had a better man working there.

"You had a handful of men, Colonel, but how many

cows? I'm sure you didn't leave the cattle from all those burnt out homesteads along the Pecos for the Comanche."

"Yes, I took the cows," he yelled as he slammed his hand down on the table. "Unfortunately most of them were so underfed and scrawny they didn't make it anyway."

"Not if you drove them across land as barren as what I just passed through."

"That rough terrain stopped the Yankee horse soldiers too."

"You're still a wanted man. They'll hang you if they find you."

"You're wanted too, Paul Quinn. You were a part of our outfit."

"Oh, am I?" I growled speaking low with a fire to my words I hadn't used yet against my former commander. "Molly McCall, or someone who knew her, passed through those Union horse soldiers with my dead body in the back of their wagon. That's what the Yankees think and they run Texas now. I'm a dead man. I can't be a wanted man too."

"Lies, damn lies, Mrs. McCall did what she had to do to get you away from the Yankees. If anybody shot you it was the Comanche. I told you that already."

I watched him close, my hand on the short barreled hideout gun I'd pulled on Ringo. Carter Brantley could be unpredictable and he was certainly prone to violence. I had no doubt he had another weapon hidden somewhere. He gave up the Navy Colt far too easy.

"Look Pecos. Maybe somebody did shoot you. Maybe it was even one of our men. When we rode up to your place Comanche were everywhere. They were shooting and we fired back. Right after we got there they broke and ran."

"I thought they were already gone when you got there."

"When I personally arrived they were gone. They'd run from our lead unit."

"Led by Sergeant Ringo, I assume."

"Yes, I believe it was." He drained his brandy glass again. Pete topped it off.

"Where did you live before the war, Brantley?"

"I had a ranch near Houston."

"A grant for helping free Texas from Mexico, I expect."

"Yes, I was there at San Jacinto."

"Good for you, Colonel. That must have been fine land. Even the Yankees couldn't take it from you. So why on earth did you come way the hell out here to this dreary place?"

"The Yankees didn't see a difference between us and Quantrill's raiders."

"But we didn't make war on innocent civilians like him and Bill Cunningham."

He spun in his seat until his back was to me then swilled the brandy again. "We didn't do the things they did, but after the Yankees broke up Quantrill's band some of his men fled to Texas. They joined our unit. At the time I was glad to have them. We were in a bad way. We needed men, and they were damn good at what they did."

"Ringo," I hissed and my hand tightened around the hilt of my hideout gun.

"He was one of them."

"Damn you, Brantley. You brought this turmoil down on all of us."

He whipped back around to me, his expression angry, hard. "Face it, Pecos, we'd lost half our force. We were losing the war. We needed all the help we could get. I had no choice."

"Because you let Quantrill's men into our unit the Yankee's were after us. I lost a wife and son," I yelled, wanting to pull a Colt and plug him, but I held back. I don't know why.

"I lost my ranch too. I didn't have a wife, thank God, but I gave up a lot."

"A Yankee general named Wallace agreed with General Walker in mid-March to end the fighting in Texas. We could have gone home then," I threw my facts at him like a Bowie knife.

"That deal went out the window the next day. Both sides were fighting at a place near Brownsville. It didn't matter much to me. The Yankees were coming after us. We could fight, flee or give up. I chose to run. Still I gave every man a choice. You wanted to stay on your place as I recall. A lot of the men along the Pecos followed your lead."

"And where are they now, Brantley?"

"You and Dodd are the only ones left."

"And Dodd is off his rocker. He's as crazy as a loon."

I got up and went over to my sorrel. "Why didn't you just shoot him too?"

"We took him with us. A number of the men in our unit broke during that action, not just the men who lived along the Pecos. There must be a dozen in the hotel along with a several women and a kid or two. I wanted to take care of the ones we could."

I wondered if I should ask him about the boy but then thought better of it. Instead I asked something else. "Is one of those women Esther Mallory?"

His eyes got big. "You know Mrs. Mallory, do you not?"

"I knew her."

"She's at the Brantley Diner," he said as he stood. "Go see her." Then he walked out.

2

Pete stood there with the brandy in his hand, stunned that his boss had left so abruptly. He poured what he could into my glass though I had only drunk a small sip of the amber liquid. "You'll take your horse when you leave, won't you, Pecos?" he pled. His face carried an expression akin to that of a beggar asking for alms on a Houston street.

"For an old horse soldier, Pete, you sure seem scared of them."

"It's not the horse that scares me. Colonel Brantley has given express orders that only his men can bring horses into town. Even the whiskey goes to his ranch and is carted here in one of his wagons. No one in town is allowed to keep a horse. I'd be careful if I were you."

"You don't say. Maybe it's Colonel Brantley who has developed a fear of horses, or maybe of horses ridden by the wrong men."

"He's always telling us that sooner or later the Yankee cavalry will come for us."

Pete said it in a completely honest way. I understood a little more about the people in Brantleyville now. They were isolated from the world around them, and that world had changed. The war had been over for five years. Colonel Brantley may still be a wanted man but today there were bigger fish to fry. I doubt if anyone else, except for me and maybe a few more men who'd once served under him, would still be looking for Carter Brantley after all those years.

Then I remembered Andy. It seemed he was acting as the sole sentry along the road into valley. If Brantley was truly worried about Union cavalry riding him down he would not trust one lone young boy to guard against them. Brantley badly wanted to keep these people here, so much so that he was willing to feed, house and clothe them to do it.

I took the reins to the sorrel and urged him toward the swinging bar room doors.

Just before we got there Pete rushed up. "Can I have my shotgun back, Pecos? I won't be shooting you, swear to God."

"Why do you even have the damn thing? You never shot anyone during the war."

"You can't ever tell. The Colonel worries some of the men at the hotel will get rowdy."

"You mean like Dodd did when I talked to him?"

"Oh no, I mean worse than Dodd. That was pretty normal for him."

So Brantley wasn't worried about the Yankee cavalry as much as he was about the men he'd stored in the hotel. Did he keep horses out of town so these men couldn't ride out into big wide world and tell someone what Brantley was doing and where he was hiding?

I handed Pete the scattergun. "Be careful with it, Pete. I don't think you should be shooting any of the men around here, except for maybe Ringo and those like him."

He took the gun but his forehead suddenly wrinkled up like I'd hit a sore spot. "There's a lot like Ringo out at the ranch. Sometimes I'd like to shoot one or another of them but I don't."

"Brantley would have you skinned if you did, I suppose."

"He sure would, Pecos. I've been with him since the war started too. He can be hard to understand sometimes. Still I have to take him at his word. This is best for all of us here."

"Yeah, Pete, maybe you have a point. Maybe this is best for you."

"Ride around back of the diner. There's a shed where you can keep the horse."

"That's good to know, Pete, thanks," I said and with that the batwing doors shrieked loud as the sorrel and I walked into the burning hot, dry air of the valley. I led the horse down the steps to the street where I pulled off my hat and swabbed my sweaty brow with the sleeve of my shirt. Then I mounted and rode slow and easy to the building next to Pete's saloon.

Like the other two structures in town it was equally unremarkable, a one story clapboard place with faded whitewash on the sides and a tall false front along the street. A sign over the main door said simply *Diner* and I wondered where the Brantleyville part went. It seemed like everything else here was branded with the Colonel's moniker. It looked lived in though, with curtains on the windows and flowers in pots near the door.

I rode around back, taking things slow and easy. I wanted to give the impression everything was under control after what I'd done earlier when I shot at Brantley's horses. I had a feeling that he'd left some of his men behind when he rode out of town a short while after our chat. They would be in the hotel now, eyeballing me like hungry hawks from the windows.

I found the shed around the corner of the diner a little before the three steps that led up to a small back porch. It had one end of a wash line tied to it with a number of dish towels flapping in what little breeze blew through here. I led the sorrel inside. There I found an empty water pail. After I ducked under the dish towels I walked to the well where I drew a bucket full of water and poured it into the pail. Then I carried it back to the shed and left it beside my horse. I heard his snout hit the water before I even stepped out into the fierce sunlight.

After bounding up the steps to the porch I walked through the open back door and looked around an empty kitchen. A large pot boiled on top of an iron stove and a pot roast with all the fixings sat on the table in the center of the table, ready to go into the oven.

"Esther, Esther Mallory," I called then pushed open the door to the dining room.

"Oh, you startled me," said a thin, pretty woman with long, plaited brown hair.

"I'm sorry. I didn't mean to. You're Esther Mallory aren't you?"

She looked me over from head to toe. "Do you plan on using all those guns here?"

I managed a smile. "I don't think so. I'm Paul Quinn. I hope you remember me."

"Paul?" she asked. "I thought you were dead. I...I'm not sure what to say. You could be Paul. You even look a little like him, but I just don't know."

"That's my problem too. There is so much I don't remember, but now that I've seen you I can remember how you and Blake would come by our homestead for Sunday supper on so many summer evenings. I even remember how he looked now. He was a handsome man."

"Paul," she said again and smiled. "Yes, yes, those were the good days before the war came and all the men went off to fight. I'm so glad to see you after all these years. How on earth did you find this place? I don't even know where we are. No one ever comes here."

She took my arm and turned me around. "Come into the kitchen. I bet you're hungry. It's been so long since I've seen you. You look, well, like you've had a wild life for the last few years. I have some eggs and potatoes I can fix for you pretty fast. Will that be all right?"

She walked next to me talking nonstop. I can't remember the last time I was this close to a woman. My whole body was on edge. Everything about her felt new and exciting. The smell of her hair, the softness of her fingers on my arm, the gentleness of her voice all intermixed to remind me of the days when all our lives looked bright. In that short time between Comanche raids and the onset of the war our days were full of hard work but through it all we held close to a warm hope of a bright future and a large family.

"Are you all right, Paul," she asked. "Here, sit down at the table. You seem distracted."

"So many memories are flooding back to me. I guess I'm overwhelmed. I saw Paine Dodd earlier in the saloon. He seemed strange. He warned me to leave this place."

I heard the sizzle of oil in a skillet and soon I smelled salt pork frying but my eyes were locked on her backside as she worked over the stove. It had been so long since I saw a woman cooking a meal, much less one for me. I'd lived on food I cooked myself, usually on a campfire somewhere far from any hint of civilization.

I caught the pungent odor of an onion and I knew Esther was chopping one and would add it to my meal. Occasionally I would pluck wild onions if I were lucky enough to find them but that was rare and this meal, as simple as it might once have seemed, would be a real treat.

"Paine certainly has his problems," she began. "When his wife and daughter died he lost his grip on life. Most everyone in the hotel is much the same as him. I managed to survive the attack but Blake was killed. I understand how Paine feels. I'm still sorry for him."

"Dodd told me that it was white man's gunpowder that killed his family. Then he warned me to take the boy and get out while I can. He sounded totally normal. Then he threw a chair and began to rage. It was like he was two different people."

She'd turned to look at me when I mentioned the boy. "Did he tell you about that boy?"

"No, he didn't, not really. Why, is there something I should know?"

She took in a deep breath. "Everyone here has memory problems, Paul. Most of us just don't want to remember what happened that day. Others, like you, were bad hurt and maybe that explains things. I wasn't at home. I came back about the time Colonel Brantley did. Maybe I was lucky but somehow I don't feel that way. It was a terrible loss for everyone."

She didn't answer about the boy. I tried a different track. "Brantley gathered up all our cattle and drove them here, didn't he?"

"He couldn't leave them for the Comanche."

"Did you see an Indian, even a dead one, anywhere along the Pecos on your way here?"

"No, but none of the women did. We heard about them from the soldiers."

I could smell the onion cooking now. It was a wonderful aroma. It reminded me of home, my wife and boy and suppers in the warm house I'd built for them. "That smells great, Esther," I told her. "It's funny how an onion frying can remind me of those early days along the Pecos."

She reached for a towel like the ones hanging on the line outside and wiped her hands. "I know how you feel, Paul. I can't tell you how many times I've yearned for those days."

"But you're still a young woman. You don't have to stay here. You could find a new life back in Texas easy. There are hundreds of men looking for a woman like you."

"No, Paul, I can't leave. I know you're right but the people at the hotel need me. I can't just walk out on them." She quickly turned back to the stove and I could hear her as she sniffled.

"That's admirable of you, Esther. You always were the selfless one."

She dabbed at her face with the cloth in her hand then turned back to me. "That's very kind of you, Paul," she said softly.

I took what she said to heart. I remembered how she was always the one who gave of herself when something happened to someone in our small community south of here. She was there when Mattie gave birth to our son. It had been a difficult birth but everything was fine in the end. I always thought I owed that one to Esther. She did the same thing when Dodd's daughter was born, and when Phil Gray was bad sick she pulled him through. She was always helping someone and now she had a hotel full of what appeared to be old friends in a bad way. She wouldn't leave here, not unless they all went with her.

"You're right, my recollection does seem better. It has to be because of people like Dodd, Pete and now you that has brought back all these old memories. For so long they were lost. Maybe I just didn't want to think about it."

"You aren't the only one, Paul. That hotel is full of friends who don't think about it."

"How about you, how is your memory?"

She wrung her hands together and looked away. "I'm no different. We all want to forget that day." I could hear her sniffle again.

"You say you want to forget it. I want to remember it. That's why I came here."

She turned back to the stove and I heard her scrape the potatoes from the skillet. Then I heard the crack off fresh eggs and with it came a smell that went straight to my gut where it worked up my hunger. I began to salivate like a dog over a fresh bone with plenty of meat on it.

"Your food will be ready soon," she said.

I realized she'd changed the subject. Was there something she didn't want to recall, or could it be that she knew what everyone else wanted to forget?

She set a cup of coffee down beside me, a worried look on her face. "I don't think talking about what happened that day is good for anyone. It will only cause trouble."

I looked up into her brown eyes. "Trouble for who, you, me or maybe for Brantley?"

"Is that why you came here, to make trouble for the Colonel?"

"I don't know why I came here, other than to find the missing memories."

She turned away and I heard her scraping my eggs from the skillet. She put the plate in front of me and took a seat beside mine, a cup of coffee in her hand. "I don't know what went on then. I'd been visiting Mrs. Meadows. She was ill with a fever. When I got home, after everything was over, Brantley told me about it, but he didn't have to tell me the effect it had on the people I knew. They were in a terrible state, all of them. They'd lost everything they had, and everyone they loved. Even me, I'd lost Blake and the home we built." She dabbed her eyes.

"Brantley was strong however. He gathered us together and made us press on. He said we'd die if we didn't. Many of us, including me, would have preferred death at that point. I was actually jealous of you. I thought you'd already gone to the land beyond, the heaven that we'd all been promised. But maybe you're in a worse hell than anyone. I have no idea. But these people are suffering every single day of their lives and I can help them, at least a little." She mopped at her face with the cloth in her hand one more time then took a sip of coffee.

I didn't know what to say to her. I took a fork full of the fried potatoes and onion and ate them greedily. Then I had some eggs. "This is fabulous, Esther. Maybe you do help them. If people can look forward to a good meal they'll keep going and if they do that then there's hope."

She looked hard into my eyes. "Do you think there's hope for these people, Paul?"

"I haven't seen most of them yet but I came here to find that hope, or a road out of the darkness. So many pieces are missing. After Mrs. McCall passed on I drank. All the whiskey ever did for me was add to the numbness that already surrounded me. Then I got a job as a scout for the Yankee horse soldiers fighting Comanche. I'm good at it. All that killing sobered me. The Yankees know where Brantley fled. They don't care about him. I do. That's how I found you."

"But the Colonel says—"

"The Yankees will be here soon. You have to be ready."

"You talked to him today."

"He sent me to you."

"Why?"

"I don't know."

"You said you don't drink."

"I said I'm not a drunk anymore."

"Don't drink the whiskey."

She caught my attention. Dodd drank the whiskey.

Ringo and the boys drank it, but Brantley had his own French brandy. Was there more to that than just the quality? "What's wrong with the whiskey," I wondered.

"I don't drink, never have. Maybe it's just my hatred of the stuff. Blake drank you know. It almost ruined our marriage. It would have if he hadn't died. But this stuff is different. I can't explain it. I guess I don't understand it. But I watched it change every one of my friends who drank it and all of them in the hotel drink plenty of it."

"And so now you're the only one in this town who can do the kinds of things most people do every day of their lives. Is that what you're saying?" I barked so sarcastically it surprised me.

"I...I don't know what I'm saying, Paul. I shouldn't have brought it up." She got out of her chair and walked to the stove, wringing her hands together like she'd done before.

Her reaction shocked me. I was used to rough men who would fight if offended, men who didn't take guff from anyone. I'd been short with her like I'd been with them and now I'd insulted a beautiful, sensitive woman who really did help a lot of people. "I'm sorry, Esther. I shouldn't have said that. It's not you and what you do here that I should be attacking."

She dabbed her eyes again then turned toward me. "No Paul, you're right. They should be able to take care of themselves. I understand what happened to them but this is a cruel world. Similar things happen to people all the time and most of them survive and some even thrive. I've often wondered what would happen to them if I were to leave."

"But you aren't going to leave are you?"

"No, it doesn't matter what the reason. They need me. I can't go."

"You're a good woman, Esther. You've always been good."

She smiled weakly but that effort seemed labored and forced somehow.

"At least you can face the reality of the situation here, unlike Dodd or Pete Conroy, who both seem to work under a false view that their daily lives are somehow normal. Yet I can't help but wonder if they are normal, at least for them. There are many things here beyond my reach."

"Why did you really come here, Paul? You say it's to find your memories but isn't there more to it? You have more guns strapped on you than any man I've ever seen. You came for war, not peace. That was you shooting at the Colonel's men in the street. Why did you do that?"

I picked up the coffee cup and took a slow sip, hoping for a little extra time to come up with an answer for her. It didn't work. I put the cup down. "I don't know why I shot at those men. I told Ringo to send Brantley alone. When he showed up with the gunmen I was mad."

"So you showed them who the boss is."

"I got to talk to Brantley alone."

"Did it help you?"

I looked down and shook my head. "I don't know that either, except that Brantley sent me here to talk to you and that has helped a lot."

"But you still don't have any more answers than you had when you rode in?"

"None that I can wrap my mind around."

She sat down again and her soft brown eyes found mine. "I know you, Paul, at least the man you were before the war came. You loved your family and your land and I'm not sure which came first. You fought to protect them both, first from the Comanche and then the Yankees. I don't know what happened to you after you realized you'd lost everything and everyone you cared about but I do know you aren't about to take a room in the Brantley Hotel and spend your days drinking whiskey in the saloon here at the Colonel's expense. Why don't you go out and spend time with the boy. I assume you saw him on your way to town. He needs you."

"The boy needs me? Why would you say that? Sure, he's young. He needs grownups around but why not you? Why not Brantley? Where does he live anyway, in the hotel?"

"He stays out there along the road. He's got a horse with him and rides into town every night and I give him a bag of food. He used to stay here, but he was too much for me to handle. He hates Brantley and I don't blame him. He needs a strong man in his life. I do what I can but there's no one else. I'm afraid he'll fall in with some of the gunmen that work for the Colonel. He's at the age where men with guns seem strong and powerful."

"He liked my guns, and he likes his horse. I talked to him some. He took me around the rock to his shelter. Then he warned me that Ringo and his crew were coming. I had no idea he lived there. Maybe you're right. I'll ride out and see him. Can I take him some food?"

"Yes, you most certainly can." She hopped to her feet, grabbed a burlap bag and started filling it with cans and jars from her shelves. "I have pickles and eggs here. A fresh loaf of bread, salt pork, dried beans, canned peaches and a few fresh vegetables from my garden."

"Esther, this is mighty nice of you," I told her as she put the bag on the table next to me.

"Oh, it's nothing. I've done this for Andy for a year at least. I'm happy to do it for you too, but please talk to him. He needs you more than you know."

I couldn't help but hear the urgency in her voice. It matched the feeling I'd had about the boy when I'd come across him on the trail. Then there was Esther. She knew more about him than she was willing to say, and about Brantley too. I stood. "I'll be back." I said.

She walked right up and threw her arms around me. "It was great to see you again."

3

I hung the food bag from the sorrel's saddle horn and rode out toward the rocks where I'd first seen Andy. It was part of the ring of rocks that formed the walls of this valley and separated it from a similar one on the far side where Brantley's ranch was located, or so I'd been told.

However, my mind, indeed every part of me from my toes to my soul, was on Esther. It wasn't so much that I haven't talked to a woman like her since I'd lost my family at the end of the war. I wasn't too darn sure if there were any more women like her. She had a remarkable ability to understand the needs of others and I found myself hard put not to expose my innermost thoughts to her right off, even if I felt deep in my heart they might scare her right out of her skin.

I knew I wouldn't be able to stop thinking about her for quite a while. At least she asked me to come back with the offer of more food an explicit, if unsaid, part of the bargain. I would return to the diner, hopefully many more times. I'd bring the boy and we could all talk. Somehow, between the three of us, maybe I could get to the bottom of this puzzling situation. There had to be an answer to what happened to so many people I had known so well for so long.

But no matter what Esther Mallory or the boy knew and might someday tell me, deep inside I was sure that the only person with all the answers to what happened along the Pecos River was Colonel Carter Brantley. This had been his brainchild from start to finish. Did his plans go awry? Did Comanche warriors interfere with his retreat and kill many of my friends and my family, or did something far more sinister happen? Something I could not yet imagine.

As I neared the rock where I'd seen the boy earlier I could make out the yellow straw of his hat as it contrasted with the dark rock. He sat in the same barely shaded spot and I knew his eyes would follow me as I rode up.

When I got within easy earshot he stood and waved his hand wildly back and forth. "Hello Mister," he yelled.

"Hi Andy," I called back.

He scampered down and ran up to me. "You're alive. Mr. Brantley or one of his guys didn't shoot you. You're real lucky." He sounded excited and happy.

"I'd rather be lucky than good, son. I brought some things from Esther. She suggested I stay out here with you for a while. Do you mind if I visit a spell?"

"Heck no, me and Willow, we get right lonely sometimes. You're awful welcome."

His broad grin made me feel special. I gave him back as broad a smile as I could muster. "How about we get this sack of food put away where it's safe."

"We'll take it back to the spring. I got a good place back there to keep it, come on," he told me and then he was off, scampering across the rocks ahead of me.

I got down from the sorrel at the stream and let him drink his fill of the cool spring water while I also settled down and drank what I needed. Andy hid the canned goods and stuff in jars on a ledge inside the cave and we put the salt pork in a canvas sack and buried it under several large rocks in the cool water of the spring.

"I got to go back and make sure no strangers come, Mister. Colonel Brantley will still tan my hide if some saddle tramp sneaks up on him at the ranch."

"Do you mind if I go with you?"

"Shucks no, I'd welcome the company. I told you I get lonesome out here."

"Then how come you didn't stay with Esther?" I asked as I trailed him through the rocks.

He stopped and looked back. "Mrs. Mallory's been great to me. I love her like she was my own ma, but she ain't. Brantleyville's the only place I can remember living and it seems like all the people here are half dead already. And worse, I'm the only kid in the whole dang town. I never knew that was special until one time she told me about the place where we used to live and all the kids that were there for a guy like me to play with. That's when I started to get lonesome. It didn't get any better when I came out here but at least I didn't have to deal with all those loco grownups from the hotel."

"I guess it must be tough on a boy like you to grow up without any friends your own age. It looks like you're coming along pretty darn good though. You're almost a man now and you'll make a fine one, I'd say."

"Do you really think so, Mister?"

"Yes, I really do, Andy. Maybe that's why Esther sent me out here. A boy needs a man in his life as he gets older so he can learn the tricks of the trade, so to speak."

He grinned wide, from ear to ear as we used to say when I was his age. "That sounds great. I'd like to learn all those tricks from you."

I beamed back at him. Somehow being with the boy made me happier than a honey bee in clover, I liked him a lot. "Well, if we're going to be friends you can call me Pecos like the others who know me."

"Pecos, wow, what a great name," he said sounding all excited. "Esther said that I used to live along a place called the Pecos River. She won't talk about it much but I always think what it must have been like to grow up by a river. That's maybe one reason I came to stay here."

"The Pecos is a lot bigger than this little brook, but it's good to live by running water."

"Can you take me to see that river one day?"

I pulled up his hat and mussed his hair a bit. "We'll

have to see how things go around here, Andy, but we might be able to make that happen."

"Why is it you came to Brantleyville, Pecos? A lot of the other saddle tramps wanted to kill Mr. Brantley. Is that what you want to do?"

That question caught my attention in a hurry. I didn't know thirteen year old boys could be so serious. "How do you know they wanted to kill the Colonel?"

"Most talked about it right off, like when I saw you earlier, they'd just say it. I guess that's why I thought you were different." He gazed out toward the small stream with a dreamy look in his eyes.

"Does Brantley live down that stream?"

"Yes sir, he has a big adobe house in a grove of fat cottonwoods down there."

"How many cows does he run?'

"I can't say for sure. Once in a while there's a saddle tramp that's not here to kill Mr. Brantley. Instead he wants to steal a steer of two. When Mr. Brantley catches him he kills him."

"What does he do to the ones who want to kill him?"

"Ringo usually shoots them."

That didn't surprise me a bit. "Ringo has killed a few saddle tramps then."

"Five or six just since I been guarding things out here."

"That's a lot of men with a grudge against Brantley." I said, still staring down the creek towards Brantley's place and wondering if I came here to kill him too. I honestly didn't know.

"Some of those guys talk about the Pecos River, like something happened there they didn't cotton to very much and they figured it was Mr. Brantley's fault. Do you know what happened to them, Pecos? After all folks must call you that for a reason."

"You're powerfully sharp for a kid your age, Andy. To tell you the truth something did happen at the Pecos River after the war, something bad. I came here because I don't remember exactly what it was or why it happened. You help my memory some and so does Esther. When I talked to Brantley earlier he was like a stone wall, no memories came in or out. Right now, I don't know what to tell you about anything that happened after the war."

"All those saddle tramps talked about something that happened after the war, Pecos, so you remember that much. I reckon that's a start."

"I guess it is," I agreed and felt a warm, comfortable feeling deep in my gut. The boy was good for me. "Maybe after sundown we could ride out to Brantley's place and scout around."

His eyes lit up. "You mean secret like, so Mr. Brantley doesn't know we're there."

"Yeah, secret like, do you think we can do that?"

"That sounds like fun," Andy said with a chuckle but then he turned serious. "Mr. Brantley has guards all over. They'll shoot us if they see us."

"Maybe I should go alone. I don't want you shot."

"No!" he screamed. "I want to go with you."

"Well, I suppose I could show you how I used to sneak up on the Comanche."

"You snuck up on the Indians."

"You bet I did, I was a scout for the Yankee's after the war. That was my job."

"You fought with the Yankee's?" he asked and I heard the anger in his tone.

"Well, after the war I came home and found the Comanche raided my cabin, killed my wife and son and ran off all my stock. I'd fought Comanche before I fought Yankees. My side lost that war and, when you think about it, all I really knew how to do was fight. The Yankees were looking for men to help them get rid of the Comanche. They didn't ask too many questions so I signed up. I have to give those Yankee horse soldiers credit. They learned a lot from us during the war and, with more help from a lot of men like me, they finally put those Indians in their place. I don't reckon the Comanche will cause Texans much trouble anymore."

"So you helped the Yankees and they whooped the Comanche?"

"Me and some other good Johnny Rebs," I said with a reassuring smile.

"And you'll show me how you snuck up on the Indians so the Yankees could beat them."

"If you've got the talent for it, not everybody has it you know."

"I got the talent," he yelled stomping his foot defiantly as he did.

"Well, that's good to hear. I'd sure hate it if one of Brantley's gunmen put a lead ball in your gizzard just because you made too much noise sneaking up on him."

"Nobody's going to shoot me in my gizzard," he said a little calmer now.

"I reckon you may be right about that. If you're sure, then I guess we can go."

"You're just teasing me ain't you?"

"Nope, I said you could go and I meant it."

"I mean about getting shot in my gizzard."

"What makes you think that?"

"People ain't got gizzards."

I yanked his straw hat off again and mussed his hair. "You're pretty smart, Andy."

4

THE SUN HAD BARELY SET BEHIND THE MOUNTAINS TO the west when Andy and I rode out of the camp headed alongside the small stream that would lead us to Carter Brantley's ranch house. A few early stars had already popped up in the darkening sky. If I understood Andy well enough we should get there around moonrise tonight, provided Willow could keep up with the sorrel.

As it was we made good time. The trail was flat, straight and easy to follow even in the dark. When we got closer to the house more and more cows came to the stream to drink. Except for a little mesquite scattered among the sage there was little vegetation and I suspected the cattle often hid in the shade of the rock from the nearby ascending rocky ridge that separated this valley from the next one that held the town of Brantleyville.

The moon was still in hiding when another stream ran into the one we followed thereby doubling the volume of water running toward the ranch house. Cottonwood trees began to appear along our path. As yet we had seen no sign of armed gunmen like Ringo and his two pals that Andy told me would be guarding Brantley's home.

"Pecos," Andy whispered. "The barn's to our left along this new stream."

"Where are the guards," I wondered.

"They ride around the cottonwoods, looking for people like us."

"How far is the house from here?"

"Not too far, a quarter mile maybe."

"Is there a place we can hide the horses?"

"You bet, over in the rocks to the right. The trees grow right up to them there."

"Let's go."

We reached the rocks as the moon rose. The added light was both a help and a hindrance. Brantley's house would be easier for us to find but his gunmen could also see us clearer as we crept through the cottonwoods. I didn't plan on walking right up to the front door however, so we tied out mounts and headed off.

We stopped before leaving the shelter of the rocks. "I want you to follow me and do exactly as I do, Andy. We're going to walk softly and not make any sudden moves. Keep a sharp eye out for Brantley's guards and listen carefully for horses or any other sound that could be from a man. The worst thing that can happen to us is for someone to see us before we know they're there. Then we're helpless. They can shoot us easy. Do you understand?"

"Yes sir, I think so."

"Don't think so, know so."

"I know so," he said softly but with a snap to his words.

"Okay, here we go." I started towards the nearest cottonwood.

We moved together from tree to tree. After a while I could see lamplight from the windows of the ranch house. About halfway there I heard a horse coming. I grabbed Andy's shoulder and put my finger to my lips. He understood right off. The hoof beats grew closer until I could see the shadow of the rider against the light from a window. I'd kept my hand on Andy's shoulder. I could feel him tremble. The rider passed within ten feet of us but rode on.

We waited until the sounds of the horse faded. We moved to the next tree and the one after that until we were close enough to the house that I could get some idea of its layout. Then Brantley passed by the window in what must be the main room of the large one story whitewashed adobe hacienda. Ringo followed him only a few steps behind. I wanted to sneak up to that window and listen to what they had to say, but not with the boy. We needed to leave. I'd done what I planned. I'd located the house and scouted a route to it. I could come back later.

I put my finger to my lips again and pointed to a

cottonwood we'd just come from. Andy understood at once but looked unhappy that I wanted to go back. Still, he followed orders.

Soon we were back at the rocks and our horses. "You did real good, Andy. I'm proud of you," I told him quietly as we led our mounts out of hiding.

"Thanks, Pecos. It was fun slipping up like that but when the rider came by it got scary."

"And dangerous, he might've shot us if he knew we were there."

"Holy smokes, I'm sure glad he wasn't looking our way."

"You're right. He looked for men riding in from the barn it seemed to me."

"That's the way the main road to the ranch house comes. I think there's another town out that way somewhere. Anyhow, that's where the food and other things comes in on a wagon."

"Have you been to this town?"

"Oh, no sir, I've never been anywhere but Brantleyville, but I been thinking on it."

We mounted and headed up the creek to the camp. Andy had a good point. There had to be a place close by where the Colonel got his supplies away from any nosy eyes in Brantleyville. "So Andy, help me out here. The supplies come in from some town outside the rocks somewhere. Here on the ranch they're reloaded onto another wagon and sent down to Brantleyville along the same trail I came into the valley on yesterday."

"The wagons come here just like you did, Pecos. As far as I know that's the only way a wagon can get into the valley," he told me with a lot of sureness.

I gave him a questioning look. "And you know that's the only way in or out of that valley because you've looked for another way?" I asked.

He burst out in a big grin. "Early one morning me and Willow rode down the other side of those rocks where we just left the horses. Nobody saw us and we wound up late in the day right back where my camp is. There's only one way into Brantleyville for a wagon."

"And that's likely one big reason Brantley picked this place," I said half to myself.

"Is that important, Pecos?"

"I don't know what it means, son. Something feels wrong somehow, like Brantley is hiding those folks from the rest of the world."

"Esther once said that she thought he was hiding everyone here. I don't think she meant to say it though cause when I asked her why she said it she told me not to worry about it."

"Did you worry?"

"Yeah, I reckon I did. I still do."

"Maybe you had a reason."

"Gee, do you really think so, Pecos?"

"I'm worried about it. Tomorrow I'm going to ride over to that town you say is out there somewhere and see what I can find out. I want you to stay here. If Ringo or any other riders come out from the ranch tell them I rode out of here early and didn't say anything to you."

"But that's not true. You did tell me where you're going."

I looked straight across at him. His eyes were locked on me and he honestly didn't want to lie for me. I had to admire him for that, but I knew it wouldn't help my cause. "Esther taught you well, Andy. She put some real character into you. Could you see your way clear to tell them that I rode out early in the morning and didn't tell you where I was going when I left."

He thought about that for a while before he broke into a grin. "As long as you don't tell me that you're going into that town when you leave tomorrow then I reckon I can say that."

"You're a fine boy, Andy. Esther must be real proud of you."

Now he looked confused. "She didn't want me to come out here. She said I was foolish."

"Women are like that, son. They want the men in their lives to be safe and well fed. She worries about things that can happen to you out here all by yourself."

"Is that why you came here?"

"She asked me to, but I wanted to get to know you better anyway. I'm glad for it."

I saw him look down. It was too dark to see his face clearly but I supposed he was shy like most boys his age. "Heck, Pecos, I ain't anybody special."

"You are to Esther."

Now his head pivoted to me. "Really," he asked in a way that said he'd not known.

"She's been taking care of you for most of your life. Didn't you realize she loves you?"

His head went slowly back and forth. "No, sir, I thought I was too much trouble."

Now I had to chuckle. "There's no reason both those two things can't be true you know. You probably are a lot of trouble for her. You're getting to the age where you want to make your own way and she still wants to coddle you, but that's because she loves you. It's hard for her to let go, just like it was hard for you to leave and come here on your own."

"You sure know a lot about me for a fellow I only met today." Now he sounded riled.

But I kept smiling. "I was your age once too you know. I wasn't so different."

"Are trying to tell me you are just like me?" he snapped and now I was sure he was hot.

"No, not at all, I'm telling you that all boys grow up to be men and while different things happen to them, the process is pretty much the same for all of us. One day maybe you'll have a son and he'll go through the things that you went through at the same age. Then you can give him some comfort when you say we all have a lot in common. That's what I'm telling you."

"I guess it's hard for me to think of you when you were as young as me, Pecos, but I guess you were once," he said in all sincerity and thereby made me feel forty years older.

"Well, thanks a lot, junior. That was right kind of you," I shot back.

His face turned sad and he looked away. For a good while he was quiet as we rode on. Then finally he turned back to me. "I guess maybe you're right, Pecos. I was mean to you just like I was mean to Esther. I don't know why I did it, but I did and I feel real bad about it."

I nodded to him, a smile across my face. "Sounds a lot like you're growing up pretty darn fast. You'll be fine, Andy. There'll be more bumps along the way but you'll bounce over them."

"I hope you're right, Pecos. I thought my meanness had to do with this place and the people in it. They all seem…well, heck…I've never known anybody else, except you, but folks here in Brantleyville are all real strange—except for Esther."

"That might be another reason Esther wanted me to talk to you."

A serious look returned to his face. "Do you think the folks at the hotel are like other people outside this valley, Pecos?"

"I only met Paine Dodd, Pete Conroy and Esther. That's not a lot to make a judgement on. But I'd say Esther is one special woman. Paine Dodd was my neighbor once. Now he's changed. He's changed a lot. And I really can't say much about Pete Conroy."

"What happened with you and Ringo?" he asked.

"What makes you think anything happened between us?"

Now he looked down and I could feel a sadness that

came over him. "He usually kills saddle tramps that come into the valley."

"And your question is why didn't he kill me?"

"Yes sir, I reckon it is. He's killed thirteen men who wandered in here like you did."

The number thirteen slapped me across the face. That many people were scratched off the sign. Was Ringo publically showing off his kills to the people of Brantleyville? "I met a boy when I got here. He shared his shade and water with me and warned me about riders that were coming. I took that warning to heart and was ready for Ringo when he showed up at the saloon."

"Ringo will still want to kill you," he said solemnly.

"I suppose so. What do you recommend I do?"

"I don't know, Pecos. I don't want to see you dead though."

"I agree with you there, my friend. But it looks like we're back at your camp. What do you say to us getting these horses settled for the night so we can get a little sleep ourselves?"

"Yeah, that sounds good." He jumped down from the mare and started removing her saddle. When he got it free he spun back to me. "Be careful tomorrow, Pecos. Brantley's men go into that town you're going to all the time. You might run into Ringo there."

I pulled the saddle off the sorrel and left it by his under the overhanging rock. Then I put my hand on his shoulder. "Thanks again, Andy. That's twice you've warned me."

"I don't want anything to happen to you. Ringo is real mean."

"Anyone who killed thirteen men is trouble. Now let's get some sleep. Good night."

"Good night, Pecos," he said as he crawled into his bedroll.

5

A pink glow on the horizon to the east told of the coming sun. I got out of my blankets and rolled them up then quietly saddled the sorrel. Andy still slept soundly a few feet away. I led the horse around the rocks before I mounted and rode off along the trail that had brought me into this valley.

As I went I kept my eyes on the ground ahead. The tracks I left when I came here stood out against much older ones of both horses and wagons. Shortly I came to the narrow gap in the ring of rocks that enveloped this valley. Beside the trail sat a large pile of dried out sagebrush that had been cut and abandoned. From here on a path wide enough for a wagon switched back and forth several times as it rose to the top of the hill, but there were no more tracks from anything but my horse. Did someone wipe any tracks they made clean when they came here?

Above me more rock climbed higher towards the

sky on both sides, but there the trail began its descent to the flat plain. Again it switched back and forth through the boulders until we reached the mesquite dotted prairie below. From here on there was no trail at all.

But I had come this way, following the words an old man who lived along the Pecos had shared with me a while ago, after he'd invited me to partake of an excellent supper cooked by his daughter. I'd asked him if a Colonel Brantley and the Thirty-ninth Texas had passed his way at the end of the war. He didn't have a hair on his head but his full beard and mustache made up for it. He was a master gunner who'd lost a leg at the second battle of Sabine Pass early in the fall of '63 when the Yankees sent gunboats and barges full of troops to attack Fort Ross. The old man was proud of the way his unit had beaten the Yankees back before the troops could land.

He told me how he'd first thought that Brantley's Texans were rustlers. He remembered how they pushed a herd of scrawny cows in front of them and had a handful of women trailing behind in a wagon. All of the soldiers told tales of Comanche warriors and Yankee cavalry close behind them. He'd been skeptical from the start.

It had been Carter Brantley himself who'd invited the gunner to the hidden valley that became the location of Brantleyville. When the old man had declined the Colonel's invitation to join him Brantley had extended the offer, saying he needed good artillery men whether they had one leg or two, and told him how to find the place. Blessed with more sense than hair the good sergeant stayed put on a fine homestead worked by a stout son-in-law and his wife.

It was planting season and that meant a lot of work for a Texas farmer. I stayed on for three weeks and during that time the memories had begun to stir in me and one of the first was that I once had a place similar to this one. Planting season must have been about the same for me then as it was for Sergeant Lankford's son-in-law. It all seemed very familiar.

The work relaxed me while I did it but come nightfall the memories pounded against the inside of my head, trying to escape from the dark confines there, but without luck. When I finally left the nightmares ended but I knew the memories were still trapped inside me. Carter Brantley, or someone with him, could well hold the key to unlock them. Lankford's directions had been spot on. I'd recognized the vee-shaped notch in the rocks as soon as I saw it.

And now I rode out of that notch and into the brush until I came to the trail I'd followed when I came here. I turned north. The rocks that bounded the valley where Brantleyville stood were on my right. At some point nearby the ridge that divided that valley from Brantley's ranch intersected it. Soon I should see tracks to the passage that led through the rocks to his spread.

The day had heated up quickly. The sun sat just above the eastern horizon while black vultures circled lazily against the blue sky a bit farther north. In a little more than a mile I saw tracks that headed off to the east, towards the rocks. Wagons and horses had been this way, a lot of them. This must be the way to Brantley's ranch. I turned the sorrel into the sun.

Before long I came again to the rocks. The tracks turned north, parallel to them and so close I could now ride in their shadow, a welcome relief from the bright sun that had been in my eyes. The vultures were now just off to my right. An offshoot of the rock ridge stuck out before me in a way that would cut across the tracks I followed but as I got closer the trail turned right to parallel this offshoot. Then they quickly veered left and led into a narrow gap a little wider than a wagon. Sumac bushes grew thick to my right.

If Brantley had guards this is the place they would be.

I stopped the sorrel and scanned the sides of the passage, looking for any sign of someone above me with a rifle. If Brantley wanted to keep me off his property he just might have his men shoot first and ask questions later, but I saw no sign of anyone. I'd been in similar situations scouting Comanche. They were much better at hiding among rocks than an ex-rebel soldier.

A horse whinnied from somewhere down the gap. The sorrel answered. Hoof beats came this way. I rode behind a small boulder that would give me some cover if whoever was coming had trouble on his mind. Then the horse came into view. He was a nice looking buckskin, saddled but without a rider. I looked up at the vultures again. They circled above me.

The horse stopped nearby. I rode over and took his reins. "Let's see what's under those buzzards, fella," I said to him and we rode off through the rocks. It didn't take long before I saw the man lying on the ground in the middle of the trail. As we got closer both horses balked. My sorrel reared up and the buckskin tugged at the reins. A few vultures still circled overhead. Others perched on the rocks around us, waiting for the man to die.

Then I heard a rattle off to my left. I dropped the reins to the buckskin and drew a Colt. The snake was coiled a few feet from the man on the ground but his interest was me and the two horses. I fired. The fanged head splattered. The long body jerked back then flopped on the ground dead. I scanned for more snakes. I didn't see any so I got to the ground and hurried to the downed man, keeping a tight grip on the sorrel's reins.

I bent over him and asked, "Are you alright?"

He groaned. "Leg...probably broke," he muttered in a pained voice.

"Did the snake bite you," I wondered.

"Don't think so. Scared my horse. He bucked me off."

"Your right leg looks busted for sure," I told him. "If you got the stomach for it I can try to pop it back together. It'll hurt like hell. Then I'll splint it and we can get you some help."

He stared hard at me for maybe the first time. "I know you from the war maybe. Yeah, you're Captain Quinn. I'm Murphy. I was in your troop," he told me in a breathy voice.

"Yeah, Murphy, I remember you, a fine soldier," I said reassuringly, but, in fact, I didn't recall him at all. Yet I knew I had to gain his trust. Somebody on the ranch would have heard my gunshot. Riders could be on their way even now.

"I don't suppose you have any whiskey do you?" I wondered.

"No, the Colonel won't let us drink on the job."

"Good for him, but we'll have to do this the hard way. Are you game?"

He grimaced. "I broke the other one during the war. Paine Dodd set it. I lived through it."

"You got guts, Murphy." I carefully straightened out the leg and watched as he gritted his teeth. I knew it would soon hurt a lot worse than it was now. I pulled on his lower leg then felt it snap back into place. Murphy screamed and passed out.

I pulled off his belt and with it a large Bowie knife in a leather scabbard that because of the lack of any wood around here would have to do for a splint. As soon as I got the knife in place and secured by his belt I heard horses coming hell bent for leather up the small canyon.

I led the sorrel over to the rocks and into a nook where we both would have a little cover just in time to see five riders race around the last curve and rein in by

Murphy. None of them looked like Ringo or the two men he'd been with yesterday. Somehow that eased my mind a bit.

"Check him," a guy with a full black beard hollered in a deep, low voice.

One man jumped to the ground. "His leg is broke. Somebody set it using his knife."

"Scatter and look for the guy who did it," Black Beard ordered the rest of them.

I stepped out and faced them. "That won't be necessary. I set Murphy's leg."

"Who the hell are you?" Black Beard yelled.

"My name's Quinn. I served with Colonel Brantley."

"Captain Quinn," a rider in a dirty gray forage hat called. "We thought you were dead."

"Not yet, but it was close."

"I'm right glad to hear it, sir. My name's Parker. Murphy and I served under you."

"Yes, Parker, you were a good man," I said and again I didn't remember him from Adam.

Black Beard looked very unhappy with all our idle chatter. "This ain't the army, Quinn. I'm in charge here. Now what happened to Murphy?"

I pointed at the dead snake. "A rattler scared his mount. The horse threw him. He busted his leg. I set it for him and tied his knife there as a splint. If there's a sawbones around maybe you ought to get him there fast." I held the reins to my sorrel loosely with my right hand and kept the other one at my side, out of Black Beard's sight.

"I told you I was in charge here, Quinn," Black Beard shouted. "I'll decide what we do."

"I reckon that's just what you should do, Mister," I said. "But I'm not under your command so I'll be on my way. I only came by to keep Murphy from the buzzards."

"Hold on there," he yelled and reached for the Navy Colt slung low on his hip.

I had my hide-out gun pointing at his gut before he came close. "You know I always had trouble getting those long barreled Navy Colts into action when they were strapped low on my hip like yours is and I was sitting on a horse like you are. It looks like you have a little trouble yourself. Now, if you don't mind, I'll be riding out of here."

"I got five men, and all of them have long barreled Colts over here, Quinn. You ain't got a chance. One of us will plug you for sure."

"Now that's a good point, Mister. One of your men just might shoot me before I kill all of you. But I promise you one thing. You will be the first man here to die. Maybe you'd like to chew on that a while," I told him nice and calm, like shooting his rotten carcass was the most normal thing in the world for me to do, and at times like this I remembered when it once was.

Parker hopped from his roan and grabbed the reins to Murphy's chestnut. "I'll take him to the doc, Blackie. He's coming around. Somebody help me get him on his horse."

Blackie stared at my Colt still pointed at him. "Yeah," he said. "You take him, Parker."

It seemed to me that he'd decided showing some compassion for one of his fallen riders was better than getting shot by me. No one in Blackie's gang volunteered to help Parker, but Murphy regained his senses and managed to get into the saddle with Parker's help.

"Are you coming with us, Captain Quinn?" Parker asked me.

"You go ahead. I'll wait for your friends to leave."

Blackie stared at me with eyes as evil as those of Cain. "We ain't taking orders from you, Captain Quinn." He stressed the word captain, perhaps to show his disdain for the rank I had once earned. He struck me as nothing more than a want-to-be sergeant. Brantley must be scraping the bottom of the barrel with him and Ringo running things around here.

I wrapped the reins around the saddle horn and with my right hand I eased the long barreled Navy Colt out of the cross draw holster on my left side, and pointed it directly at Blackie's head. "Do you see how much easier it is to get the Colt out from the other side when you're sitting on a horse, Blackie. If we'd been up against Comanche your hair would be gone by now, so why don't you be a good boy and run along?" I cocked the hammer.

Blackie sucked in a deep breath then yanked the head of his horse around. "Get back to the ranch!" he yelled to the men with him, slapped his horse's rump with his hat and rode off as fast as he could. The rest of his crew followed him, but without the same level of urgency.

I caught up with Parker and Murphy near the end of the passage between the rocks. Murphy moaned a lot. His leg must hurt something powerful. I guess that's natural.

In spite of what happened to him it occurred to me that Parker was the one in trouble. Blackie got as mad as a treed polecat when he thought I was telling his men what to do, and by offering to take Murphy to the doctor Parker would face his wrath when he returned.

When I got to the trail and headed north Parker hung back to ride beside me. "I'm awful glad to see you again, Captain. Everybody thought you were dead after they found you shot in the head like you were. Things were so confounding what with Comanche and Yankees all around us. Most of us thought we were damn lucky to get away with our lives, but it made a lot of us awful mad that you got left behind like you did."

He had an honest look on his face and the act of caring enough about Murphy to get him to a doctor was a good sign. He was young, maybe not yet twenty-two with eyes that still held a fresh hopeful look in spite of what seemed like his now dangerous employment.

"How long had you been in the war before you came here, Parker?"

"Oh, not long, sir, just a few weeks," he said.

"The war was lost by then, son? Why on earth did you get involved?"

"Soldiers came to the farm. They said I had to go with them. The Yankees were coming. If I didn't go my family would lose everything. I went."

"You loved your family a lot didn't you?"

"Oh yes sir. My Mama begged them to let me stay."

"Have you seen her again?"

His boyish face turned angry. "No sir."

"You've been with Brantley the whole time?"

"To the Colonel the war's not over. If I left I'd be a deserter. He has men who would hunt me down and bring me back. He's hanged men for it, and Ringo and his crew killed a lot more."

"Was it Ringo who came to your farm?"

Parker's eyes grew wild. "Yeah, it was him," he said then spat on the ground. "If anyone on that ranch needs killing it's Ringo."

"You say Brantley thinks the war is still going. Does he do anything about it?"

"Sir, you were my Captain when I first joined up. You were about the only officer most men respected. Did you show up here today to join up with the Colonel again?" He spoke straight up and on the level but there was a quiver in his words, like maybe he hoped I wasn't here to join Brantley.

"I thank you for the kind words, Parker, but you didn't answer my question. Is Brantley planning something?"

He looked down and shook his head. "I was never anything but the lowest private in the unit, Captain, and that's all I still am. This is only the third time I've left the ranch since we got here and it's always a trip for supplies with Blackie and some other guys. But I've got eyes and I see things that don't add up. Heavily armed men leave the ranch. They're gone for weeks sometimes. When they get back a man or two isn't with them, others have wounds."

"So you think the Colonel is sending men on raids?"

"He glanced back to check on Murphy who was now a good twenty feet behind us. "I got ears too, Captain, and those men say things. My Ma was a good Christian woman. To her it would sound like these men went out to rob places, banks and maybe trains. He sent a unit out this morning. The talk is about getting Winchester Rifles and cartridges, and then we'll be ready."

"Ready for what?" I snapped.

"I don't know, Captain. I'm just a private."

"Parker, why did you stay with the Colonel after the war ended?" I asked him again.

"I told you, sir, we were still fighting Yankees. For us the war has never ended. But men talk. A couple of guys heard Lee surrendered and the South lost. They both were loud mouths according to Ringo. He took them on his next raid and they didn't come back. Now no one else talks about Lee surrendering. And according to Colonel Brantley we're still in the war."

"The war is over, Parker. It has been for five years."

He looked at me with sad eyes. "I'm not surprised, Captain."

"What are you going to do? Brantley will come after you."

"What are you going to do, Captain?" He threw my question back at me.

Parker was looking to me for answers. I was his leader when he joined the cavalry. I guess I still was. "Have you been to Brantleyville?" I asked instead.

"No sir, only Ringo and six or eight others can go there. The rest of us mostly stay on the ranch. The only reason I rode up the cut today was because Blackie was yelling at me and the other guys about letting a calf get away from us without a brand when we heard the gunshot."

"It sounds like you're more a cowboy than a soldier."

"Yeah, we need the beef to feed the men, but sometimes Brantley will drive off a herd and take them north. Only certain guys go on the drives."

"What will he do to you for helping Murphy?"

He looked at me again, fear crawling from his face. "I might go on a raid, sir."

"And Ringo would kill you." I said what he didn't have the guts to tell me.

He blanched as white as the towels hanging on Esther's wash line.

"I got the impression that Brantley wants me dead too, Parker. I had a run in with Ringo yesterday. He wanted to draw on me for no real reason. Blackie just did the same thing."

"He would have killed you and left your body for those buzzards."

I looked back over my shoulder. The vultures no longer circled over the passage through the rocks that led to Brantley's ranch. "It looks like both of us have a problem."

"Yes sir, but didn't we have a problem before?"

I gave him a knowing smile. "We certainly did, Parker."

6

A LONE TWO STORY BUILDING STOOD A GOOD WAY BACK from the trail and Parker headed towards it. Farther up the wide cow path we were riding on, and just as far back from it, sat a one story adobe that I guessed was a saloon judging from the horses tied in front. Like in Brantleyville there was no activity anywhere around. No trees or grass grew here either, only a few small mesquite and the same sagebrush I'd ridden through for days. We rode up to the two story place. A faded sign in front said *Benson's Store*. We left our horses in the shade on the north side.

A shingle hanging from the covered wooden walkway in front of the place said simply, J.B. Burns, MD, with a small arrow that pointed up the stairs beside the store. We helped Murphy to the ground. He seemed in fairly good shape in spite of the ride. We both looped an arm under a shoulder and half carried him up the steps.

A gray haired man in a white shirt, sleeves rolled up and sporting an unbuttoned gray waistcoat opened the door before we'd even knocked. "Hurry, bring him inside and get him settled on the table over there," he said and pointed to what looked more like a high, narrow bed to me.

Meanwhile, Doc Burns had washed his hands in a white bowl and was now putting on wire framed spectacles. "It's his leg I take it," he said and headed over to Murphy.

"His horse threw him," Parker said.

"Who set this?"

"I did."

He glanced at me then pulled off the belt and the knife I'd used as a splint and tossed them on the floor. "I haven't seen this trick in years," he muttered and began to feel the leg near the break. Murphy screamed, leaving no doubt the doctor had found the busted bone.

"You did a good job," he told me as he grabbed a bottle from a nearby shelf and poured a healthy dose into a glass which he gave it to Murphy. "Drink it all, son," he ordered.

Then he picked up a roll of white gauze and started wrapping the leg. "I won't need to reset this. The leg should heal up fine," he went on. "You must have learned how to set a bone in the war. Are you with Colonel Drake out at the Bar D ranch?" he asked.

Parker stepped up. "I am sir, but Captain Quinn was just passing by."

Burns stopped wrapping and looked from one of us to the other. "Not many men just happen to be riding by Drake's place, boy," he said to Parker before turning back to me. "So just what is your story, Quinn is it?"

"I was in the war, Doc. I don't know Drake but I served with Colonel Brantley and had come up to see him when Murphy here ran across an angry rattlesnake. What did you give him?"

Burns grinned. "Most rattlers are angry," he said, "but the glass held laudanum. It will help the pain but I gave him enough that he should pass out soon." He went back to working on the leg. At last he stood and turned to us. I need to put a cast on this limb. I don't need you two standing here gawking. Why don't you go down the road and have a few drinks."

"Someone else from the ranch could be by to check on Murphy, Doc. We have some things to do so we'll be leaving. You can send your bill to the Colonel, I assume." I told him

"Do it all the time," he told me but gave me a look that said he wouldn't buy what I'd just told him with Confederate money. Then he looked to Parker. "Son, I'm going to need something from the store before I finish with Mr. Murphy. Can you run down and get it for me?"

"Oh, sure I can, sir," Parker agreed.

Doc Burns scribbled something on a piece of paper and handed it to him. Parker hustled out the door and clomped down the stairs.

Burns turned to me. "Look Quinn, I don't like to get

involved in the personal business of my patients or of those who bring them in to see me, but your story about just dropping by to see Drake is as farfetched as any I've ever heard. Nobody just happens by the Bar D to visit."

"I wasn't going there on a social call, Doc. Something happened at the end of the war. Now I can't remember a lot of those years. It's strange. I see a man and I know him but I may not remember what we did together or what happened to us. Somehow I think Brantley knows."

"Brantley," he yelled. "You mean Drake don't you?"

"I mean Colonel Carter Brantley of the Thirty-ninth Texas. If he calls himself Drake now it's news to me."

"You're a fighting man, Quinn. I haven't seen a man with so many pistols since the war."

"Are Brantley and Drake the same man, Doc?" I put a hand on the grip of a Navy Colt."

"Don't threaten me, Quinn. You may need my services soon."

"That could well be, but now I need an answer. Are Drake and Brantley the same man?"

He walked over to the front window and looked out. "How did you get to be such good friends with that boy, Parker I think you called him?"

"He served under me for a short time near the end of the war."

"You remember him then?" he turned back to me.

"No, but I was his Captain. He remembers me."

He walked over to Murphy. "He's out now. To answer your question I think Brantley and Drake are the same man. I'm a doctor. I don't want to get involved but there have been rumors of shootings at the Bar D—murders that go unreported. Men talk, Captain Quinn, and when they don't know the truth they make up things. But you lost your memory. Did something happen to cause that loss?"

"Someone shot me in the head."

"That could do it, but clearly you survived."

"That seems to be a problem for Brantley."

"I've never seen a Bar D man in town with anyone else, like Parker is here with you."

"Parker is Murphy's friend. He defied an order so that Murphy would be taken care of."

The doc walked back to the window and peered out again. "Parker will be back soon. What will Drake, or Brantley, do to him for disobeying that order?"

"He can't go back there. He knows that."

"What do you plan to do?"

"I plan to live and keep Parker alive as well."

"Who shot you in the head, Quinn?"

"I don't know."

"But you suspect someone."

"I do."

"There are more men who've escaped from the Bar D. Can you come back after sunset?"

"How do I know you aren't setting me up?"

He walked over to a roll top desk in the corner and sat. He wrote something down, folded the paper in half and offered it to me. "These are three men who could give you the information you're looking for. I can have them here after dark. Leave your horses in back of the building. No one from the Bar D will be in town then. I'll keep Murphy here overnight, but I suspect he just may want to go with you when you leave tonight. Go ahead, look at the names."

I unfolded the paper and read what he wrote. "I'll be here, Doc." I told him.

Heavy footsteps tromped up the stairs then a knock came from the door. Burns opened it and Parker came inside, handing a package wrapped in brown paper to him. The doctor put it on a shelf. "Thank you, son," he said to Parker. "Tell me, do you drink much at the Bar D ranch."

"Drink sir, do you mean whiskey?"

"Well, yes I do."

"They let the men have whiskey after sunset. You can have as much as you want, up to a point I guess. I'm not much for whiskey so I don't drink it. I give mine to Murphy most nights. He gives me his hard candy when we get it or maybe his fried potatoes when we have them. There are a lot of things I like more than whiskey."

"You don't know how lucky you are son, if Murphy gets your whiskey ration daily."

"Most every day, unless he ain't around at supper time. That doesn't happen much but I can always find somebody to swap with."

"You mean you never drink the whiskey," Doc asked sounding seriously surprised.

Parker looked down like a kid caught with his hand in the cookie jar. "I don't like whiskey, sir. It just doesn't taste good and it leaves me feeling all out of sorts."

"And you act like you're ashamed for not drinking the devil's brew."

"The other men ride me about it, sir."

"If I may say so, young man, my professional advice to you is to continue avoiding strong spirits." He turned to me. "Now I need to put a cast on this patient's leg. Walk your horses to the back of the building then ride due west about a mile. You'll come to a small pine woods. It will give you a concealed place to hide with shade. I'll see you here after sundown."

"That's thoughtful of you, Doctor," I told him as we took our leave.

We left Doc's office without incident but I noticed Parker kept looking behind us as we rode away. We followed a narrow trail between clumps of sage and the occasional mesquite. I could see pine trees ahead. My gut told me Doc Burns was on the level, but I couldn't be sure.

There was something about the whiskey that bothered me as well. Burns had been awful interested in Parker's drinking habits and I wanted to know why. When I threw that in the same bucket with Paine Dodd and the folks at the Brantleyville Hotel and what Pete said about their drinking, something stank worse than a dead buffalo carcass festering in the hot summer sun.

Parker looked behind us once more. "Is anyone coming?" I asked him.

He didn't answer. Instead he stopped, turned his horse and stood high in his stirrups. "It could be riders coming, sir. I just can't tell."

"Are you expecting company?"

"Blackie will send people after me, and he knows you were there this morning so they'll come after you too."

"The doctor called Brantley Drake. Did you know about that?"

"The Colonel said the Yankees knew his name so he goes by Drake up here. Most of the soldiers still use Brantley though, but I don't get off the ranch much."

"What will happen to you if his men catch up to us?"

"I don't know about you, Captain, but I'm a deserter now. I'll be shot on sight."

"Parker, the war has long been over. You can't be a deserter. Brantley is an outlaw."

"Does that mean I'm an outlaw too?" he asked as a look of fear cast across his face.

"Did you go on any raids, steal anything or shoot anybody?"

"No sir. I never went on one of the raids. I doubt if I shot anybody since I joined up."

"I don't think you're an outlaw, but don't talk about your time on the Bar D with anyone you didn't serve with. People might not be too forgiving of a man like the Colonel."

He wheeled the roan back around towards me. "I guess nobody's back there."

"That's good. Tell me about the whiskey men were given after sundown. Were there a lot of fights and rowdy behavior from them?"

"Oh, no sir. Most drink their fill and hit the sack."

I looked at him hard half expecting to see a big grin smeared across his face, but he seemed as sober as a judge. "Have you ever spent time in a saloon, Parker?"

"No, sir, I grew up on a small ranch a long way from any town."

"That explains a lot," I said but I wasn't thinking about Parker's inexperience with the evils of drinking. "That looks like the woods where we need to spend the day."

Parker was looking back over his shoulder again. "Captain, maybe I was wrong. I think somebody is back there and coming this way."

I spun the sorrel around and took a look. Sure enough riders were headed toward us and at a fast pace too. "Come on, let's get to the trees," I said.

Before long we came up on the pines and rode into the cover they provided from the intense heat of the sun. There we stopped and once more gazed across the nearly barren prairie to see three riders heading this way. I reached into my bags and pulled out the field glasses I'd gotten from the Yankee cavalry when I helped them with the Comanche.

I didn't recognize any of the riders so I handed the binoculars to Parker. He looked for a long time before he gave them back to me. "They seem familiar but I can't place them. Maybe they were once working out at the ranch though."

"Is that Smith and Wesson six shooter strapped on your hip loaded?" I asked him.

"Yeah, and I got most of a box of cartridges too."

I pointed to a rifle butt in a scabbard on his horse. "Can you use that Sharps carbine?"

"I was raised on a ranch, Captain. I can bark a squirrel or hit a jack rabbit on the run."

"But you've never shot a man?"

"No sir, at least not that I know."

I put the binoculars back up to my eyes. "The guy in the lead, in the beat up top hat, I've seen him before," I mumbled, mostly to myself but I couldn't be sure if I knew him or not. I simply didn't remember and we couldn't take any chances, not if Colonel Brantley, or Drake if that's what he went by now, had sent these men here to kill us.

"Parker, take your horse back into the trees and tie him securely so he won't bolt when gunfire starts. Then come back here with the Sharps and all the ammo you got."

He looked out at the men riding hard towards us. "Yes sir," he said and I could swear he actually thought about saluting before he ran off to the rear with his horse in tow.

I took my sorrel back into the pines as well,

grabbed the Henry rifle and as many cartridges as I could carry and returned to the tree line. The riders were still coming fast. Parker ran up, Sharps in hand.

"Get behind that fat pine there," I told him as I pointed to a tree a few feet away. "Load the carbine but don't shoot until I tell you. They may not have anything to do with us."

"They sure look like they're after us," he said as he scrunched up against the rough bark.

He's right about that, I thought, but I'd been around long enough to know what I thought didn't mean a thing. It was what was on their minds that would determine the outcome of this encounter. And there would be an encounter, either for good or bad.

The guy in the top hat started pointing towards the tree line where we hid, almost like he knew we were here, but even more like he was planning a military maneuver to attack our position. He sent one man toward our left flank and another toward the right. Still, he only had three men and they would all be exposed if they charged us out in the open like they were. I didn't know how much help I could get from Parker but I was pretty sure I could pick off all three men in less time than it took to load cartridges into Parker's Smith and Wesson.

The three riders had spread out wide, but now they'd slowed to a walk. That made me a lot more reluctant to start shooting. "Hold your fire, Parker." I called out as quietly as I could.

A faint, "yes sir," seemed to float back on the wind, but I knew Parker understood.

I cocked the lever on the Henry, jacking a cartridge into the chamber. I was ready.

I could see them clearly now without the field glasses. They all carried a Henry Rifle in their right hand with the butt braced against their hip. They thought we were here but they weren't quite ready to fight. Then Top Hat said something and they all stopped.

"Take it easy, Parker," I whispered.

Before he answered Top Hat rode forward alone. "Captain Quinn," he called in a clear, loud voice. "I'm Miles Durant, remember. I was your sergeant."

The name rang a bell inside me. I put the binoculars up to my eyes again. His face looked familiar. The name of a place popped up in my mind. "What about Chaplin Hills," I yelled.

"We were running from the Yankee's near Perryville, Kentucky. A sniper took out your horse. In spite of all the musket fire I came back and picked you up. We both got out of there. Later you remembered me and promoted me to sergeant. We made it through the war together. That is up until we all thought you died along the Pecos."

"A lot of men thought I died on the Pecos, including me. What brings you here, Durant?"

"You do, sir. I saw you and Private Parker help a man into Doc Burns place. A little later you and Parker came out and rode this way. Are you with Colonel Brantley?"

"What if I am?"

"I don't think you are, sir. I talked to Burns before I came. We need your help."

"Help with what, Sergeant?"

"Burns gave you a paper with three names listed. My name is on it."

"Look, Durant, I just got here. I don't know what is going on."

"Ask Parker about me."

I looked over to the tree where Parker waited. He looked confused but certainly no more than me. "He used to be at the ranch, Captain. He disappeared over a year ago," Parker said.

"Leave the Henry and your two friends there then come in real slow," I told him.

He stuck the rifle back in its scabbard and slipped down from his horse. He walked nice and easy toward me with his hands out to his side. As he got closer my memories began to stir. I remembered him now. We'd served together for three years. How could I have ever forgotten?

But I knew the memories I now had were but bits and pieces of the whole story that floated in and out of my mind in a disjointed way like things from my past always did. They would be here today but gone tomorrow. Try as I might they would never stay with me.

"I remember you now, Miles, but ever since that day

on the Pecos I've had trouble with things from my past. Don't take anything I said too hard."

"This is mild compared to the war, Captain."

"What's going on at the Bar D? Doctor Burns said Brantley was now called Drake."

"I don't really know how to explain it. At first we were still fighting the Yankees. We came here after you got shot along the Pecos. A lot of other good men died that day, supposedly from Comanche attacks. I've never talked to a single soldier who saw a Comanche that day, except for Ringo. Do you remember him?"

"I met him yesterday in the Brantleyville Saloon. He tried to draw on me."

Miles Durant's eyes lit up like a lantern glowed inside his head. "You beat him to it."

"Like I would've beaten you if you'd tried anything funny."

"Look at you. You're still a warrior. You've been fighting Comanche."

"With the Yankee cavalry," I spat the words, my dislike for what I'd done clear.

"We need you to fight with us, to lead us."

"Fight who, and for what?"

"Brantley, and for whatever evil is going on at that ranch."

"We can't just declare war on a man because we think there is some mysterious evil force on his property. We need a reason that the Yankee law will respect. Otherwise we'll have to fight them too. What has Brantley done?"

"He's still fighting the Yankees. They just don't know it. His men ride for days then pull a raid on a bank or a train. They rustle cattle. They took every cow they could get from along the Pecos, the ones supposedly raided by Comanche."

"Hold on, you mean it wasn't Indians that shot me and killed my wife and son?"

"Don't you want to know what happened back then? Isn't that why you came?"

I stared straight into Miles Durant's cold blue eyes. They didn't blink. He didn't flinch.

Then the truth that had been locked inside me came out like a flash flood. "Brantley raided our homes on the Pecos," I wailed. "He killed as many of us as he could, then blamed it all on Comanche and rushed the troopers off by saying the Yankee cavalry was after us."

"You've known all along, Captain. You just didn't want to face it."

"Damnation," I moaned. Then, stunned by what had flashed through my mind, I dropped to my knees in the deep pine needles beside a tall pine and buried my face in my hands.

Parker came up and put his hand on my shoulder. "Are you all right, Captain?" he asked.

I shook my head hard then stood and held out my hand. I needed a moment. My sudden realization was either like dying or being reborn, I wasn't sure which. "Yes, I'm okay," I said once I'd gathered my faculties. "What do you want me to do, Miles?"

"We have upwards of a dozen men scattered within

a day's ride of here. The Colonel must have fifty. He's constantly getting arms and ammunition and we've got whatever we came away from the ranch with, but all of us, to a man, are willing to fight to take Brantley down."

"Is this all because of the Pecos raids?"

"Think back Captain. Remember how a small group of Quantrill's men had joined the Thirty-ninth Texas and some, like Ringo and those who came with him, began to have more and more influence over Colonel Brantley. The war was going badly. After Vicksburg we lost control of the Mississippi. We were cut off from the rest of the south. The Thirty-ninth Texas became raiders and because we couldn't get the supplies and arms we needed we became thieves. At first we stole from the Yankees but later we took whatever we could find wherever we could find it."

I turned away from him, shaking my head to clear the cobwebs. "I argued with Brantley about what he was doing. You were with me. Paine Dodd was there and several others who lived along the Pecos. We all knew the war was over but Brantley wouldn't give up."

"He made it sound so patriotic. The south would rise again and we would be a big part of that. We just needed to stay together as a fighting force and wait for the change that was sure to come. The south wouldn't tolerate the punishment the Yankees would inflict on them. Men would find out about what we were doing and flock to our flag. We would win in the end."

I slowly turned back to look full into the face of

Miles Durant. Parker was standing close by him, leaning on his Sharps carbine. He nodded in agreement with what Miles had just said.

"I remember now. Our arguments with the Colonel got intense. Our men fought among themselves over what we should do. Then Brantley came up with a compromise. We would stay together until we reached the Pecos. The men who lived there could leave and go home. The rest would continue to a place where Brantley said the Thirty-ninth Texas would be safe until the time came to rise again. Then he was sure most of us would rejoin him."

"Your memory is excellent Captain," Miles said and he was right. Things flooded back now, tumbling through my mind like water over rapids.

"I met a few people who live in Brantleyville, Pete Conroy, Paine Dodd, Esther Mallory and the boy, Andy. Only the last two seem to have their wits about them. Two of them I've known for years. Paine Dodd and Esther Mallory were once my neighbors. Esther is still the loving, caring woman she once was but Dodd goes from calm and collected to raving mad in a heartbeat. He was never like that when he served with us."

"The shock of what the Comanche did to his family caused his problems," Miles said.

"I thought no one saw any Comanche, Durant?"

"There were no Comanche, Captain."

"So what happened to Dodd?"

Miles Durant pulled at his overgrown whiskers. "The same thing that happened to you."

"Oh my God," I said as a picture of my farm flashed across my mind. My wife lay on the ground by the burning barn, scalped and raped. I'd fallen to my knees beside her when I heard the horses. I turned to see Ringo and his men ride up. Before I could react, I was shot.

"I remember now, Ringo shot me." I told Durant.

"Just like he shot Paine Dodd."

"We need to be sure of what Brantley did before we attack the ranch or we could hang."

"Yes sir, but I never thought of it that way. The Pecos raid was a crime against Texans."

"If that's the case," I said, "the Yankee law won't care."

7

THE SUN HAD ONLY RECENTLY DROPPED BEYOND THE horizon when Parker and I arrived at Doc Burns place. We eased through the twilight to the front steps. Miles Durant waited there for us. He checked the street for any sign of Brantley's men then waved us on. Soon Doc Burns ushered us inside. Murphy sat in a well stuffed chair, his busted leg supported by a padded footstool.

Parker walked over to him. "How are you feeling, Murphy?"

"Better than I was earlier. Thanks," he said. "Doc told me how much hot water you're in for bringing me here. I guess we're both in trouble with Blackie now."

I came over. "Is the doctor taking good care of you, Murphy," I asked him.

"Captain Quinn, we'd all thought you were dead, sir. I'm damn glad you showed up when you did. I owe you plenty."

"You don't owe me a thing, trooper. You just need to heal up," I said.

"Yes sir," he said then his eyes moved to Miles Durant. "What are you doing here, Sarge? When you went on that raid and didn't come back we thought you'd died too."

"Ringo tried to kill me. He missed but I'm not the only one. It's great to see you again."

Heavy feet tromped up the stairs. Doc Burns opened the door before they knocked. "Come in fellows," he said and two men walked in. They wore old, dirty gray slouch hats with what was once a yellow tasseled cord above the now battered brim. Both carried a Navy Colt.

The taller of the two walked straight to me as soon as he was inside. "Captain Quinn," he said. "It's so good to see you, sir. We thought you died along the Pecos back in Texas."

His eyes bored directly into mine as I took his hand and shook it. "Forgive me," I said. "It's been a while but my memory is just starting to come back. Would you be Sergeant Nick Farley from second platoon?" I asked him with no small amount of hope that I was right.

"Indeed I am. It's been a long time, sir. The man I came here with was also a sergeant, though he was promoted by Brantley after you were shot. This is Chuck Norman," he said as he gave a half turn and swept his arm toward his companion who stepped up and saluted easily.

"I'm thrilled to meet you at last, Captain Quinn," he

told me with a wide grin that showed his sincerity. "So many men in the Thirty-ninth Texas respected you a great deal. I'm glad you're with us. We have reason to believe Brantley is about to make a big move. We must stop him."

"Captain Quinn seems more worried about the people living in Brantleyville than he does with fighting Brantley and the men from the Bar D," Miles Durant told him.

I looked around the room. Everyone's eyes were on me. These men were here because they needed leadership. I knew I had to provide that for them. It was control of our unit that caused the final rift between Brantley and me, a fight that almost cost my life. Now we would have one more confrontation. It would decide the fate of the men of the Thirty-ninth Texas.

"Forgive me, Norman," I said as I shook his offered hand. "This is the first I've heard of a big move by Brantley, but I do feel it's vital that we rescue those in Brantleyville from whatever it is that holds them there in what seems to me to be a jail without walls."

"Pardon me, Gentlemen," Doc Burns broke in forcefully, "but I have reason to believe that the problem with the people at Brantleyville has to do with opium addiction. Your good Colonel could well be adding laudanum to the whiskey he serves the people there, as well as at least some of those who work on the ranch. Mr. Murphy here is a prime example. He exhibits the classic symptoms of an opium addict, while I suspect Mr. Parker, the man who always traded away his whiskey ration to Murphy, does not."

What Burns said brought a thick silence to the room as if no one understood what he was really talking about. The face of each man looked blank, except for Nick Farley. He held a resolute expression and seemed to have something to say. He caught my eye and nodded.

"I've been talking to Doc Burns about this since it happened to me," Farley began. "I went on a raid with Ringo and several others who were regular raiders while I'd been working the ranch and having the normal ration of whiskey at night. We didn't drink at all after we left the Bar D. By the next morning I had the shakes. As we rode on things got worse. I got the runs and had to stop a lot to go. Then I couldn't sleep. Ringo called me a malingerer and said if I didn't shape up he'd deal with me. I thought I had the dyspepsia and I'd get better pretty quick."

He looked around the room. The faces of the men were glum. Miles, Chuck and the doctor must have heard this before but for Parker, Murphy and me it was brand new. And yet somehow I knew Farley was right. That's why the liquor tasted funny in the saloon and why Brantley drank his own special brandy when he was there.

"Well, I didn't get better," Farley went on. "After the third day Ringo had enough of me. It was pitch dark but I still couldn't sleep. I heard him coming. In spite on my miserable condition I knew what was on his mind. I pulled the Henry from my scabbard and moved away about ten paces from where I'd spread out my bedroll. I was sweating like a horse and shaking at the same time. He walked up and put four shots into my blankets. Soon the whole group rode off."

My eyes were focused on Farley throughout his speech. "What you've told us makes sense, Nick. Esther Mallory and Andy don't drink and so they don't get the laudanum. That's why they're the only normal ones in Brantleyville. What would happen if we cut off the supply of the drug and the whiskey to the Bar D ranch?"

Everyone sat quiet again. Nick Farley's story had hit them hard enough but then I'd added the idea that a woman and boy had been in trouble for years because of what Brantley did. They'd lived right under the noses of these men without most of them knowing anything about them.

Doc Burns stepped to the center of the room. "I'm not a military man, far from it, but I think I know where your mind is going, Captain Quinn. In the next few days you will all see what happens when a man who is used to a daily dose of an opiate no longer gets it. Murphy here was given a good dose earlier. He'll be fine until tomorrow but then he should suffer similarly to what Farley has been telling you. Perhaps we should let Farley finish his story."

"I agree, Doc," I butted in, "but before he does I'd like Chuck to tell us what this big move Brantley is about to make will be and when we can expect it."

Chuck stood and looked over to Farley who nodded at him. "Ringo, the Colonel, and way more than a dozen of his best men rode out of the Bar D this morning heading north. The word I get is they plan to raid a shipment of Winchester Rifles heading by train to California. If this is true and they pull it off they'll have enough firepower to make them unbeatable to us."

"So we have to stop the Colonel and free the people in Brantleyville pretty fast," I said

Parker stood. "I told you about this raid earlier, Captain."

I nodded to Parker then gazed around the room. The face of every man here was resolute. They were good soldiers in their day and now they were willing to go into the fray one more time. "All right, Farley. I'm sorry I interrupted. Let's hear what happened to you."

"I was in a bad way when Ringo left, but I'd been damn lucky that he didn't kill me. Still I was too sick to ride. I thank God he was in a hurry and didn't take time to check and see if I was dead. I stayed where I was for days. I don't really know how long. I had a little food in my saddle bags but everything I ate either came back up or ran out the other end. My stomach hurt. I shook all the time. I was always hungry but mostly I craved more whiskey. But it must have been the laudanum I wanted. After about a week I started to feel better. I had no place else to go so I came here and went straight to see Doc Burns. He sent me to Miles Durant and here I am now."

"So, the week or so you were sick, is that what we

can expect if the men at the Bar D lose their laudanum?" I asked, hoping between Burns and Farley I could get a reliable answer.

Burns shrugged. "I can't say for sure, Quinn. It may depend on the amount of the opium a man has been taking and the length of time he's used it."

"Would you say Murphy here is typical of a Bar D hand?" I wondered.

"Sure, I'm just like the rest of the men," Murphy said.

This time Burns shook his head right off. "No, not if what both he and Parker says is true. Murphy traded for Parker's whiskey. He had as much as twice the laudanum as the others."

"I guess we'll find that out soon enough," I said. "And how long after your last drink of laudanum laced whiskey did it take for your troubles to start, Farley?"

"We didn't have any whiskey that first night and not long after that I started cramping up and wanting a drink. The next morning I had the runs and was starting to shake."

"Would that be what a normal man could expect, Doc?" I wondered.

Again he shook his head. "I have no way of knowing. Everyone could be different."

Miles Durant stepped forward. "Look, all this talk about whiskey laced with opium is interesting but we need to know if you're with us, Quinn, and then we need a plan to take care of Colonel Brantley and his men." He looked directly at me. "So what do you say, Captain."

As strange as it seemed to me now, what with all the serious talk of what could well be a bloody range war with the men of the Bar D, I found myself smiling. "Sergeant Durant, you may now assume that I am your commander. I need detailed information on the unit reportedly sent from the Bar D ranch for the purpose of commandeering arms. Plus I need to know where the Bar D obtains its supply of laudanum. I plan to coordinate our attack with a withdrawal of this drug, thus disabling a number of their men. One of my highest priorities is the safety of all civilians in the town of Brantleyville. This is a big task, gentlemen. Are you up to it?"

A cheer went up from everyman in the room. The smile on my face dropped straight into my heart and was replaced by an old military bearing that I'd long thought lost.

"Sergeant Durant, organize our withdrawal from here at once."

"Yes sir! Parker, Murphy and the Captain will be quartered at my ranch until further notice, if that is acceptable, sir?" he said with the snap a good top sergeant always had.

"That will be fine," I replied.

Doc Burns walked up to me as the men began to leave. "The Bar D gets their laudanum from the same place I do, Captain, downstairs at the general store. I'll help you work out a sudden shortage without raising suspicions at the Bar D. Come back when you can."

"Thanks, Doc, for everything you've done. I'll be here soon."

"My pleasure, Mr. Quinn, after all, taking care of those around me is my calling."

Murphy struggled to his feet. "Will you help me down the steps, Parker?" he asked.

"Sure buddy, I'll be happy too."

Doc Burns grabbed a pair of crutches leaning against the wall and gave them to Murphy as he stood. "Take care of yourself son. You'll have a rough week or so but always remember that this is the only way to get rid of the drug in your body."

"Thanks for helping me out, Doc. What do I owe you?"

"You don't owe me a red cent, Murphy. I'll send a bill to the Bar D Ranch and hope I get paid before you guys do whatever you're going to do."

"Murphy gave Doc Burns a confused look. "But didn't Brantley go north with Ringo?"

"Don't you worry about it, Murphy. I want you to be strong, and I'll want to know what problems you have. The men at the ranch may follow in your footsteps."

"Thanks Doc, I'll do what I can to help."

"I know you will, son. Now be careful with those stairs."

A wagon was waiting for Murphy in front of Doc's place and soon we headed north. At last Miles Durant veered from the rough trail we'd followed and turned east into the endless prairie. Finally we came to a small pine woods much like the place I'd met him earlier. I could see several small adobe buildings with sod roofs and a slightly bigger barn also with a sod roof but whose sides were made of small branches nailed parallel to the ground that allowed ample air to flow through for some tiny bit of comfort to the animals inside.

"Captain," Miles called as we pulled up in front of that barn. "You can stay in my cabin, sir. Murphy and Parker, you'll be in the bunkhouse. Breakfast is at sunrise. I'll see you then."

Parker took our mounts and Miles and I walked off. "So this spread is yours?" I asked.

"For what it's worth, yeah, I started here after I got away from Brantley."

"Doesn't he know you're here?"

"I don't know. I don't go to that saloon much and I don't think Brantley ever does. Starting a fight with me wouldn't be in his best interest anyway. It would attract attention."

"Or maybe he was just waiting for those new Winchesters."

"That's a good point. The idea that Brantley is so close to me does keep me up at night. When I came here I didn't think much about it. My problem was with Ringo, or so it seemed, but as time went by I began to put things together. You were a big piece of the puzzle. The people in Brantleyville, we could put them up here in just a few days if you want."

I spun to look into his face as we walked across the dusty ground. "If we get them here quickly enough maybe a few could help us against Brantley and his men when they show up."

"Maybe, but I don't even know who is there, except for Paine Dodd. He was a good man once. Will he be able to fight in a week or two?"

"I don't even know if Doc Burns can answer that question."

"Maybe we don't have to move them anywhere," he said, "if you cut off their laudanum at the same time we do it to the men at the Bar D."

"Do we have the men to look out for all these people for as long as it will take? Then what happens if the Colonel comes back with Ringo and his best men while we're busy?"

"Then we'd be in serious trouble, Captain, with our force split into at least two places and playing nursemaid to a bunch of helpless opium addicts we'd be dead."

"I agree, Sergeant. I'd like to get the boy and the woman out but unless the rest of the residents leave I don't think Esther Mallory will go. Maybe at least I can bring the boy here."

"Won't that tip off the men still at the ranch?"

"Maybe, but they won't know he's here if no one sees us."

He opened the door to his cabin, struck a match

against his trousers then walked in and lit a lantern. "Come inside, Captain. Make yourself at home."

"Thanks Miles. For a Thirty-ninth Texas veteran this place is terrific," I told him.

"It beats the hell out of a canvas tent in the middle of a cornfield."

"That's for sure."

8

I'D SPENT THE DAY WITH MILES DURANT, SETTING UP our upcoming plans against Carter Brantley. He'd put all the men on his place to work erecting another adobe building in anticipation that one way or another we would need it. I wasn't convinced that would happen but it kept them busy and that was important for their morale. Now, the early evening stars lit the darkening sky as I rode past Doc Burn's office on my way toward Brantleyville.

I had to see both the boy and Esther Mallory one more time. I very much wanted to take them away from the evil in that town and out of the reach of the Colonel, but deep in my heart I knew Esther wouldn't leave. As long as there was even one person there who needed her she would stay. She seemed driven to help those in the hotel and they did need her. It was a part of her nature, a trait I found incredibly attractive, but right now it was also terribly frustrating.

Andy was a different story. I knew she cared a great deal for him. She'd raised him until he'd gotten too old for her to handle. He'd moved out to live by the cool spring near where I first saw him, but she still made sure he had plenty to eat and did the best she could to keep him on the straight and narrow. I would take him to Miles Durant's ranch. There he'd have a lot more people to interact with, but unless Esther came with us there would still be no women there.

The men with Miles Durant were not cold, cruel gun hands like Ringo or Blackie. They'd invested a lot of their lives in the war and were now trying to make the best out of whatever was left for them. There had been no parades for the losing side, no medals or official appointments in a government controlled by outsiders. There were no jobs to speak of because there was no money to pay a man. The ranchers had land filled with wild cattle, but cows were everywhere in Texas and that meant they were almost worthless.

Men had begun to drive these animals north to the new railroads that would ship them to St. Louis or Chicago where they could be processed for sale to hungry easterners. In 1866, soon after the war, two men, Charles Goodnight and Oliver Loving, had driven a herd of longhorns from Fort Belknap in central Texas up the Pecos River, over the very trail I'd come here on, to Fort Sumner where they sold most of them for eight cents a pound.

The next year they tried again but were attacked along the Pecos at Horsehead Crossing by Comanche and the herd scattered. Loving went ahead with another man to inform the fort's soldiers of the delay but was ambushed and wounded. He died soon after.

If what I'd heard was correct, Goodnight had now driven herds into the Wyoming Territory town of Cheyenne where they could be shipped directly to Chicago on the Union Pacific Railroad and then, perhaps, even farther east.

At Doc Burns office last night I'd been told how Brantley had sent a fairly large group of his raiders to steal weapons being sent west on that same Union Pacific line. They would certainly be guarded by well-armed men or even Yankee troops who would not part with them easily. The implications of his success were huge. The Colonel would have a force better armed than the Union Cavalry that I'd spent the last few years scouting for.

I rode past the entrance to the Bar D ranch where only yesterday the buzzards had circled over a wounded Murphy waiting in their impatient way for him to become their next meal. The narrow passage through the rocks was a wonderful natural defensive fortification, but only if the invaders didn't know about the side entrance that Andy had led me through on the way to his shade and cool water camp site.

With the last glow of twilight, I passed through the notch in the rocks and came to the place I'd first seen Andy. He was nowhere around. I took a chance and called his name but got no answer. I rode on towards town. I wanted to see Esther as well as the boy and she would hopefully know where he was.

It was full dark when I got to the diner. The lamplight glowing in the windows led me to believe someone was there. I rode to the rear and left my horse. The back door was open and I could see her moving about the kitchen. I stopped in my tracks and sucked down a deep breath. It had been many years since I'd called on a woman in the evening like I was doing now. My heart pounded, pushing blood into my head. Would she be happy to see me?

Damn, I thought. Here I am acting like a school boy. I stepped onto the porch, calling her name as I neared the door. I saw her turn, surprise across her face. And then she smiled.

"Paul," she said with a voice like an angel, "I'm so glad you came. Come in."

"I had to see you, Esther," I said as I passed through the door.

She rushed to meet me and before I knew it my arms had closed around her. I looked down into her lovely face and found her inviting lips with my own. She snuggled closer into my embrace and returned my kiss with a fire I hadn't felt from a woman in far too long.

At last she pulled away and looked down. "I'm sorry, Paul. I shouldn't have kissed you like that. It wasn't proper. Please, don't get the wrong idea about me."

"I don't think I have the wrong idea about you at all, Esther, but I haven't been kissed like that since before the war." Her eyes rose and met mine. She smiled like a young girl might.

"Have you had supper," she said. "I have roast beef. It's pretty good. I'll get you a plate."

She turned to the stove and pulled out a chair at the table on her way. "Here, sit down."

I sat and waited, watching her work over the hot stove, spooning up the beef, potatoes and carrots from the black iron pot. Like the kiss, it would be a meal unlike anything I'd had since the war began.

"Have you seen Andy," I asked her.

"Not since this morning. Haven't you been with him?"

"I left him yesterday. I've found out some things. I came here because I need to take you and Andy away from here."

She put the plate in front of me and then sat down across the table. "I can't leave, Paul. The people in the hotel need me. I don't know what they would do if I left."

"Do you know what Brantley has been feeding them?"

"I've been feeding them, three times a day."

"It's opium. It kills pain. He puts it in the whiskey. If they stop taking it they get sick."

She stared at me as if she didn't understand. "I know they all drink a lot. I thought that was part of their problem but I don't know what you're talking about."

I looked deep into her soft eyes and realized she had

never heard of opium and why would she. Soldiers like me were all too familiar with pain. Rumors of the pain killing effects of the laudanum the Yankees had but we didn't spread like wildfire through our ranks.

"After I'm done eating can we go over to the hotel? I want to see these people," I said.

"Honestly Paul, I don't know why you want to see them. They don't do much. They just sit and stare or lay about in their beds. They hardly even talk."

"I guess that's part of the problem. A lot of this is new to me as well."

"The Colonel always said it was the shock of what happened along the Pecos when the Comanche came that caused their problems."

"I don't think the Comanche raided our homesteads. I think it was a part of the Thirty-ninth Texas. There were no Yankee cavalry after us either."

She sniffed and reached for a napkin to wipe her eyes. She was crying. I had no idea why.

"Carter Brantley wants to marry me, Paul. He's not a man to take no for an answer."

I stared hard at her, shocked at what she'd said. "Don't you understand? He sent Ringo and some other men to raid our homesteads and kill our families. Then he took the survivors here and fed them opium laced whiskey so they would forget what happened. He's a ruthless murderer. You can't marry him." It had taken all my self-control to not yell at her. How could she not understand what was happening here?

"I guess I've known all along that it was Ringo and

his crew that raided our homes Paul, but for a woman like me things like that lose their importance after a while. Carter would get me away from the people in the hotel. I would have a life again, with more finery than I ever thought I would have. He promised to get me anything I want, anything at all."

"Esther, he can't buy self-respect for you. Think about what you're doing."

"It's been so long, Paul. I've lost hope."

"That's because there is no hope here in this so called town. It's a jail, a prison without bars filled with the half human remnants of people we once knew. There are more men out there. Most escaped from the Bar D ranch after Ringo tried to kill them. Maybe, if things work out, we can get rid of Carter Brantley entirely. I plan to cut off the drugs those in the hotel are getting. They'll get terribly sick for a while. I don't want you to have to deal with that."

She stood and spun away from me. "I've been taking care of them since the beginning. I can't turn my back on them now."

"But you can turn your back on me?"

She slowly faced me again. "If I must, Paul," she said as the tears started to fall like rain.

I stood. "I want you to go with me to the hotel. I want to see the people there."

"No, Paul, you don't want to see them. They drink all day. They're passed out by now."

"I assure you, Esther, I've seen worse than anything at that hotel. I went through the war. I've been in hospitals where the arms and legs of good men were piled up like firewood. I've gone into Comanche villages after the Yankee horse soldiers rode through and killed all the men and raped all the women. The people in that hotel deserve their life back. There are more men on Brantley's ranch that he's gotten addicted to opium as well. They deserve a chance to live. But most important of all are you and Andy. You deserve a life away from this place and I came here to see that you get it. I want to take you both away tonight."

She leaped to her feet and spun around leaving her back to me again. I saw her dab at her face with the napkin. Then I heard the sniffles. I got up and quietly walked behind her and gently put my hands on her shoulders. She leaned into my chest and my arms wrapped around her.

"Take Andy with you," she said. "He'll be here soon. He missed you today. He worried that Brantley caught you. He doesn't know that Ringo would kill you. I couldn't tell him."

"I can't leave you here. Either I take you away or I'll have to take everyone in the hotel."

She pulled my hands apart and turned to look into my eyes. "You can do that?"

"I think so. Some of the men on the Bar D are fed the opium in their whiskey too. I'm going to cut off the supply. That will make all of them as sick as a dog for a week they say."

"I'll go with you if you take them. They'll need my help more than ever."

"What would they do without you?"

"Carter would have killed them all, at least the ones in the hotel."

"Will he notice if I take Andy away?"

"Carter's gone. I don't know where. He's never left like this before so it must be important. He plans to marry me when he comes back. He'll be a powerful man then, he says."

It was a question I had to ask. "Do you want to marry him?"

She didn't flinch but stared straight into my eyes. "I don't have any choice."

I took in a deep breath. "You don't have to marry him if you don't want to."

"He'll kill you if you interfere."

"He'll kill me anyway."

"Oh, Paul, you need to get away from here before Carter returns. Take Andy and go back to Texas. He won't follow you there. He's a wanted man."

"I can't do that. There are men here who escaped from the Bar D. A lot of them were in my troop. They need my help. Carter Brantley will kill them too."

She pulled me close and put her head on my shoulder. "We're two peas in a pod, Paul. Both of us are trapped here because of Carter Brantley."

"I need to see the people in the hotel. Would you go with me?"

"Andy will be by soon. I should be here."

I nodded. I wanted her to stay here and take care of the boy. She'd been the best person in his life so far. I hoped she would continue to be important to him. I pulled from her arms. "I'll come back here after I see what I need to. If Andy shows up keep him around."

She smiled in a comforting way. I knew she was the rock that Andy rested his life on. She would do as I asked and if I took him away she would be more inclined to go with me next time.

I walked out the back door and up to the front of the building. A vast canopy of stars filled the sky above me. Except for the lamps from Esther's kitchen I could see no other lights anywhere. The hotel across the street was completely dark. The front door stood half open. I stepped into a lobby even darker than the starlit night outside and stopped to let my eyes adjust.

After a while I could see a man sitting in an overstuffed chair with his head on a table in front of him. It must be the effects of the laudanum, I thought. A lantern sat on a nearby table. I picked it up and realized it was still warm. Someone came by here and turned the lights out after the residents were asleep. Could that be a part of what Esther did to take care of these people? I wanted to believe it was.

I struck a match, lit the lantern then turned the wick down low. The man in the chair looked familiar though his hair was long and hadn't seen a comb or brush in years and his curly beard hung down below the edge of the table. I looked at him for a while, wondering if he was once my neighbor or perhaps one of the troopers in my command. I had no answer and walked away. No one else seemed to be down here so I headed up the stairs.

A man slept in a chair by the front window, a half empty jug sitting on the floor next to him. I went down the hall planning to check each room. In the first one there were four beds with a man in each. The next was much the same. A third had only two people in it while the fourth held three women in one large bed. No one woke when I shined the light in their face. Not a single person even stirred. They were all in a very deep sleep. I went back to the man by the front window and shook his shoulder with enough force to wake even a normal drunk. He didn't respond, instead continuing his deep slumber.

I headed down the steps to the lobby, holding the lantern high to make the most of the dim light from the short wick. The man still slept with his head on the table. Nothing looked different since I'd gone upstairs but I put my hand on the Navy Colt in my cross draw holster just to be sure. Then I carefully looked around the room. I caught movement off to my right and drew the pistol, cocking the hammer with my thumb as I did.

"Take it easy, Paul. It's Paine Dodd." He struck a match and soon another lamp glowed.

"Everyone's asleep. Why are you awake?" I asked.

"Like Esther I don't participate in Carter Brantley's ruse. If you recall I never drank, even under the pressures of the war. I don't make a habit of imbibing the swill in the saloon here either, but I do find it useful to give the impression I'm drinking it once or twice a week. That's what you saw me doing the other day. I also thought I warned you to stay away from here."

"You did warn me, Dodd. I took it seriously."

"Then why did you return?" He took a step back after closing the lamp. For the first time I could see his face clearly. He looked deadly serious.

"I'm not completely sure," I told him, "but I do want to get Esther and Andy out of here."

"And Esther won't go."

"Not unless the people in this hotel go too."

The hard expression on his face eased. "And Brantley will have you killed if you try."

"I really don't know the answer to that, Dodd."

"But you're willing to try."

"I have an idea. I don't know if it will work or not."

He sat down in a nearby chair and put his hand on his forehead. "His men will kill you."

"I heard he was gone and he's taken Ringo and most of his gunmen with him."

Dodd's hand came down and he looked at me with interest. "Where will you take them?"

"There's a place not too far from here."

"And how will you take care of them? Who will feed them all? Can you do all this?"

"There are men out there who were once in the same shape as the people in this hotel. They've come back from what Brantley did to them. They live a normal life now."

"And do you think the people here can do that?"

"I don't know, Dodd, but they won't be able to stay here much longer."

"You're going after Brantley. He'll kill you for sure then."

"It's what Brantley has on his mind that will cause his downfall. He's planning on stealing a shipment of repeating rifles to use against the Yankees. He wants to start the war again, or at least get rich robbing Yankee banks and trains. If he does they'll hunt him down."

"I remember those repeating rifles from the war. We said the Yankees could load them on Sunday and shoot all week."

"Why are you still here, Dodd, pretending to be like the rest of these people?"

He walked to a window and stared out. "I suspect we aren't so different, Paul. We both homesteaded on the Pecos. We fought Comanche because we had to and then the war came. We served together until the end. Then we both just wanted to go home." He turned to me, his face seemed eager for some sign of agreement from me.

"That's the way it was Dodd. But our real problem began on the Pecos."

"But we went down different roads. I saw Ringo and the men with him shoot my family. I went after them but someone jumped me from beside my burning barn. They beat me senseless. When I came to the rest of the troop were there. They told me how lucky I was that a Comanche didn't kill me too and how sorry they were about my family. At first I thought maybe I'd been seeing things. It really wasn't Ringo's squad that killed my loved ones. After we got here I started to realize that something was wrong. Some men disappeared. Others changed fast. It didn't take long to see that the whiskey was behind that change. I was never a drinker. I decided that I needed to play along or I would disappear too. What you saw two days ago was an act."

"You put on that show for Pete and I got the feeling then that you'd done it before. But why didn't you take Esther and the boy and get the hell out of here years ago?"

"You know the answer to that. Esther wouldn't leave. She won't leave with you either."

"How does the whiskey get here," I asked him.

"Men from the ranch bring it once a week. The last load came three or four days ago."

"If I can find a way I'm going to stop it."

A wide eyed look of fear crossed his face. "What will that do to the folks here?"

"They'll get sick, but in the end they'll recover and won't need what's in the whiskey."

"I'll help you, if you let me know when."

"I'll do what I can, but there are more men than me involved."

"I'll be here when you're ready," he said.

Even in the dim light I could see his smile. It struck me that it was something rare for Paine Dodd at this point in his life.

Outside the sound of a horse could be heard.

"Andy just got back to Esther's," he said. "Go and see

him now. Take him away with you tonight." It sounded like an order. He'd told me the same thing at the saloon. Both he and Esther wanted Andy out of Brantleyville and it wasn't hard to understand why.

"I'll take him tonight. Then I'll be back later for the rest of you."

9

I crossed to the diner and went to the back door. Andy's mare waited tied to the stair rail. I gave her a pat as I walked by. Inside Esther fussed over something on the stove. Andy sat at the table having supper. He spun in his chair as soon as I walked in.

"Pecos," he called, then hopped up and ran over to me. "I missed you."

I put my arm around his shoulders. "I missed you too, Andy. How've you been?"

"I snuck onto the ranch again just like you and me did the other day," he said.

"I told you not to go there, Andy," Esther snapped as soon as she heard him.

"Aw, heck, Esther, it's no big deal."

"Well, maybe it is, Andy," I said. "I've been hearing an awful lot of things today and I think Esther's right. I also found some old buddies of mine who are starting a new ranch not too far from here and they could sure use some help. I'd like you to come up there with me. They don't have anybody like Ringo or Blackie who shoot people on sight. What do you say, want to go?"

"Yeah," he yelled, excited to get away from Brantleyville like any boy would be.

"That's great. There are some real good men there. You'll like them."

"Finish your supper, Andy, so you two can get going before it gets late," Esther said as she wiped her hands with a white dish cloth.

"You bet, Esther. You know how much I like beef stew." He sat back down and started in again on his meal and from the speed he was eating he really did enjoy it.

I sat beside him. "We'll pick up your stuff when we get to your camp. Is there anything here you need?"

"Not that I can think of. I can always come back if I remember something," he told me like coming back was no big deal but I noticed how Esther tensed over his comment. She knew that even for Andy returning here would be dangerous.

I caught her attention easily. "I'll take good care of him, Esther. Don't worry."

Andy hopped to his feet. "Esther always worries but I'm ready to go, Pecos."

"Isn't there anything here you want to take," I asked him again.

"Nope, I took it all to the creek," he said and started for the door.

"Aren't you going to say goodbye, Andy?" Esther asked while she walked around the table towards him.

He stopped and turned to her, smiling wide. "Sure, Esther but don't worry. I'll be back to see you lots of times."

She wrapped her arms around him and then kissed his forehead. "You listen to what Pecos tells you and do what he says. I'll miss you. Remember I always want the best for you."

"I know, Esther. You keep telling me that." Then he turned and ran out the back door.

"I'll take good care of him, don't worry," I told her.

"I can't help it. I've raised him since he was just a boy."

I saw the tears in her eyes, walked over to her and took her in my arms. "I'll be back for you as soon as I can. Stay strong."

"I will," she said. I kissed her deeply then followed Andy outside.

Once on the street I saw someone watching us in the dim light from a first floor window of the hotel. It had to be Paine Dodd. I hoped I could count on him when the time came.

We worked our way through the rocks to Andy's camp. It didn't take long to gather the few things he had there and soon we were off. Back on the trail we passed the Bar D ranch and then the store with Doc Burns office upstairs before we finally arrived at Miles Durant's place. Lamplight shone from his small, lone front window.

When we dismounted at the cabin the door opened. Miles came out with a rifle in his hand. "Hi, Andy," he said. "I had a feeling I might see you tonight."

"Miles, wow, the guys at the Bar D told me you bit the dust but I'm sure glad to see you alive and kicking. Is this your spread?" Andy sounded happy to see him and that should help a lot. One more body in that small cabin was pushing things. It would be good if we all got along.

"You bet, it's my place, Andy, and I'm darn pleased you're here. Come on in. Are either of you hungry?" he asked as he ushered us inside.

"We ate at Esther's," Andy told him.

"Make yourselves at home. I'll see to your mounts," he called as he closed the door.

The next day I was up before the sun but wasn't surprised to see Miles sitting in front of an open fire and working on breakfast. "Good morning," I said. "Where's Andy?"

"Morning, Captain. He's checking on his horse," Miles answered as he poured coffee and handed it to me without asking.

"Thanks," I said and sat on a stool. "I talked to Paine Dodd last night. He seemed normal and told me he's been playing along with Brantley. He wants revenge."

Miles looked over. "And you trust him?"

"I don't know whether to believe he's free of the laudanum or not but everyone else in that hotel was asleep. He wasn't and he said he would help us if we took the people away from there. Esther Mallory won't leave until they go."

"But she wanted you to take Andy."

"So did Dodd. I want to get those people out of there."

"We can bring them here, but not for few more days."

"Do we know for sure that Brantley is gone with Ringo and his gunmen?"

The door flew open and Andy rushed in, already excited about being out of Brantleyville. "I was on the ranch last night, Pecos. I slipped in just like we did. I heard some of the guards talking. They said the Colonel left yesterday with Ringo and some other guys."

"Andy, you need to be careful," I told him totally sure he'd slipped onto the ranch because I'd taken him with me the night before. "I'm sorry I gave you the idea."

"Heck, Pecos, it's fun to slip up on those guys and it's really easy."

"I understand, Andy, but Ringo and the men with him are apt to shoot you before they bother to find out that you're just a kid having fun. They won't understand what you're doing."

I knew he felt bad that I'd chewed him out when his smile vanished and he looked down. "I'm glad you didn't get hurt," I said. "I can use the information you told me, but promise you won't go back to the ranch again unless you talk to me first. Maybe I'll even go with you."

He raised his head and grinned. "Sure, Pecos, I ain't hankering to get shot anyhow."

"How about some breakfast guys," Miles said. He pulled a pan full of salt pork out from over the fire. "There's oatmeal in the pot. It's ready too. Molasses and butter are on the table. You guys help yourselves."

We all dug in. I found the meal Miles cooked to be excellent. After all, except for Esther's beef stew last night and a few other homes where I'd been invited to dinner, I'd lived on army cooking for nearly ten years. The boy took to Miles meal pretty good as well.

"Andy, would you like to take a ride with me?" I asked him as we scraped the tin plates we'd eaten from and dropped them in a bucket of water to soak.

"You bet, Pecos. Where are we going?" he said and his answer bubbled with excitement.

"Over to the store we passed on the way here."

"Yeah, I've never been to a store before."

"Do you think you can get our horses saddled while I say a few things to Miles?"

"Sure, I can do that right quick," he said and ran out of the house.

"He's a good boy," Miles said. "I hope what happens here won't ruin that."

"He's seen some pretty bad things in his life but he'll be fine," I told Miles. "I'm going to talk to Doc Burns about cutting off the laudanum to Brantley's people. If we can take over the ranch while most of the men are suffering then maybe we can catch Brantley's raiding party in the narrow pass where I found Murphy yesterday. They'll be trapped and all those new Winchester's won't do them a darned bit of good."

He cracked a smile. "That's good thinking but it will take a lot of luck to pull off."

"Those folks at Brantleyville could use some luck."

"That's the truth."

He asked a few more questions that I answered as best I could then I walked outside as Andy came up riding Willow and leading my sorrel.

"Good job, son. Are you ready?"

"Yes sir. Willow even seems excited to be out in the big wide world."

"Is that what you call being out of Brantleyville?"

"Esther would always tell me that one day, when I got out into the big wide world, things would look different to me. I guess I never really understood her then."

"Well, do things look different yet?"

"No sir, not so much, everything looks pretty much the same, but it sure feels different."

I had to grin. He was exactly right. The same mesquite and sagebrush that were all around Brantleyville were here too. "There's a whole lot more to this world than what you see here, Andy. When I was in the war we went all the way to Tennessee and Kentucky. There the land is full of trees and it isn't so darn hot all the time. You even get a lot more rain there, and that's still just a little piece of what the big wide world is like. But what you're feeling is called freedom."

"Holy smokes," he said. "Esther wasn't just pulling my leg."

I checked my saddle and tightened the cinch a bit then swung up and we rode off.

After a while Andy called out. "Pecos, I was wondering if that freedom thing is just not worrying about whether a Brantley man will catch me if I do something wrong?"

"I'd say that for a guy like you that's a big part of it. Freedom is a man's ability to do what he wants as long as he's not trampling on the freedom of others to do it."

"Are the people in the hotel free to leave Brantleyville like I did?"

I looked at him. "You're asking some serious questions, Andy. Those people should be able to leave and go where they want but you tell me if you think they really can."

"I never thought about it that way, Pecos. I don't think they can leave."

"How about Esther, can she leave?"

"Holy smokes, I never thought about that either. If Esther wasn't there those people in the hotel would be in trouble. I don't think there's a one who could do what she does."

"What about Paine Dodd?"

"He's different somehow, not like the others. He might be able to leave. He scares me."

That answer hit me like cold water in my face. Andy could say things in a real down to earth way. "I think you're right Andy. Dodd seems scary to me too but not like a Comanche warrior would, or even a gunman such as Ringo, but more like another man's dog that could be friendly at times yet if he got an idea you might hurt his master he'd jump you in a heartbeat."

"I guess I don't know much about what dogs are like, Pecos. There was a dog on the ranch last year but I think Ringo shot it. He likes to shoot things."

"So what scares you about Dodd?" I wondered.

"I don't really know, sir. Maybe it's the way he stares at Esther when she's not looking. Mr. Brantley does the same thing 'cept maybe he's worse. Sometimes she'd yell at him to let her go. I never heard her yell at Mr. Dodd like that though."

"Does Brantley come by the diner much?"

"A couple of times a week I'd say, usually in the evening after the hotel folks are gone."

"Do you know why he comes by like that?"

"She said he wants to marry her. Then she'd go and live at the ranch with him. She won't do it because of the people in the hotel, but I don't think she wants to live with Mr. Brantley."

"I don't think she wants to either, Andy."

"He gets real mad at her sometimes. I worry he'll hurt her."

"Why do you think Brantley gets mad at her?"

"He always gets mad when people don't do what he wants. Then he hurts them or has Ringo or one his gang do it for him."

My eyes popped open wide. It wasn't so much that Brantley had tried to bully Esther into marrying him, because that was the kind of thing he did, but Andy had noticed his behavior and knew why he did it. The boy had some savvy.

"So you've seen him do that to other people," I asked hoping for more.

"Lots of times," he said. "Is that how Brantley takes freedom away from people?"

"You know Andy, I do believe it is."

"So you have to threaten people to make them marry you and then when they do you've taken away their freedom. Is that how it works?"

I spun around in my saddle to make sure he was serious. His face was set in stone. It hadn't been what I'd expected. "You haven't met many people who are in love have you?"

"I love Esther. She loves me."

"Well, that's true with you and Esther but one of these days you're going to meet a young girl about your age and you're going to think she's the most special person in the world. If she feels the same way about you that means you're in love and she's the person you want to marry."

"I never knew a girl my age. I never knew a boy my age either."

"Some day you will, hopefully soon, now that you're out of Brantleyville."

"I hope they have more gumption than the folks in the hotel."

"I'm pretty sure you'll see a lot of folks who are a lot more active than the ones in town. Why don't we stop by that store we passed yesterday and get you some new clothes so you can look good when you meet them? Will that work for you?"

Now his eyes got really big and his smile grew to match. "Yeah, I'd like that a lot."

"There it is up ahead. Why don't you go inside and look around and see if there's anything you like. I want to talk to Doc Burns upstairs for a few minutes. We'll leave our horses in back where they can wait in the shade."

"Willow will like that. She doesn't much cotton to standing in the sun," he said.

I watched Andy as he walked up to the front, his eyes wide. He stopped and stared into the lone window at all the things that a place like this had on hand. He'd already said that he's never seen a store before and right then I decided I wanted to go inside with him.

"Maybe I'll go in with you, Andy. Doc Burns can wait," I said.

He looked over from the window. "Great, Pecos, this place looks really swell."

"They have a lot of stuff in there, but remember we just want something to wear."

"I'll remember."

I opened the door and held it for him as he practically ran inside, his head still swiveling back and forth. A short, balding man in a sweat stained white shirt with sleeves rolled up to his elbows hurried over. "Morning gentlemen, what can I get for you today?"

We need something for Andy here to wear, a shirt,

THE BETRAYED

trousers and maybe a hat." I took at peek at Andy's feet. "And a pair of boots," I added quickly.

The man scratched his beard. "We ain't got much ready-made stuff, but a peddler got stuck here a while back and left some things you might like. Maybe there's something the boy can use."

A short time later we walked out, with a shirt, pants and a hat for Andy plus a brand-new pair of Texas riding boots. The shoes he'd worn in here had holes in the soles. He was grinning from ear to ear, as happy as a fish in water.

"This is great, Pecos. I've never wore stuff like this before and the boots make me feel like I'm full grown," he said as we walked back to our horses to drop off his old stuff.

"You've got a ways to go yet to be full grown but you do look more like a man in them. I still have to go up and see the Doc. If we say anything you don't understand I'll explain it later."

"Are you sick, Pecos?"

I grinned. "No, at least I hope I'm not. It's about the people in the hotel."

"They sure seem sick," he said in his honest, down to earth way and we started around the building to the steps that went up to Doc's place.

"Doc Burns knows what their problem is. Maybe we can help them," I told him.

All at once he stopped dead in his tracks. "I don't think you can do that. Mr. Brantley said he would kill those people if Esther didn't marry him," he told me as if it were no big deal.

I stopped too. "When did he say that," I asked.

"Right before he left on the trip he's on. She has until he comes back to make up her mind. If she says no the people will all die. I guess he'll let Ringo shoot them."

"Did he say how long he'll be gone?" I wondered.

"No more than a week is all I heard clear. He's getting some guns."

Andy made it sound like someone was selling him guns. Could they be the Winchesters that I'd heard about? It made sense. But if Brantley had gone all the way to Cheyenne it would take longer than a week. Something didn't add up. "Did he know you heard this?" I wondered.

"No, I'd left Willow in the shed earlier and had been currying her then I gave her some oats when he rode up," Andy went on. "I went to the back porch and listened. They were arguing. Then she wanted him to leave. That's when he told her. She yelled at him to get out and I heard the front door slam and his horse ride off before I went in. I could tell she'd been crying but I didn't say anything about what I heard. I didn't want her to yell at me for being nosy."

"I'm glad you told me, Andy. This is very serious. Let's go upstairs."

10

Doc Burns door opened as soon as we reached the top of the steps. "Come in, Captain. I was expecting you today," he said to me but with a sharp eye on the boy.

"Good morning, Doc. This is Andy. He's been living in Brantleyville most of his life."

"How do you do, son? I've heard a lot about that town lately."

"I'm glad to meet you, sir," Andy said politely, showing off the manners Esther taught him.

Doc smiled at his reply but quickly looked to me. "How is Murphy doing?" he asked.

"Things went just like you said they would, Doc. Parker is looking after him. He put up a shelter near the outhouse so Murphy could manage easier on his busted leg and he stays with him most all day. Word is he's starting to get better."

"Good, I'll be by to see him soon. Meanwhile, I

talked to Tom Benson downstairs about the laudanum. He gets a shipment once a month and usually hauls a load to the Bar D a day or two after. That was two weeks ago." He glanced at Andy perhaps unsure how much he should say with the boy around. "You'll have to wait."

"Or come up with a different plan. I heard last night they deliver the whiskey to the hotel and saloon once a week. They must keep the laudanum on the ranch and add it to the whiskey."

"Benson said his man takes it to a small adobe near the barn. That's all he would say."

Andy pulled the sleeve of my new brown shirt. "I know where that shed is," he bragged.

I looked down at him. "You've been on the ranch a lot more than you've let on."

He grinned back at me, clearly proud of what he'd done. "A little bit I reckon."

"You're what, twelve years old, son," the Doc asked.

"I just turned thirteen, sir."

"That's an age when young men want to explore. I'm sure he finds the Bar D an exciting place, don't you son?" Doc Burns reached back to his roll top desk and picked up his wire rimmed spectacles and strapped them over his ears and onto his nose. "You look pretty darn healthy to me, young man, but in my opinion you'd be best to stay away from that ranch if you want to remain that way. There are some brutal men there."

"Oh, I know that, sir, but that's part of the fun," Andy answered with a bright smile.

"I'm sure it is but it won't be fun if you're caught," Doc Burns warned him.

"I agree, Andy," I said. "You're only asking for trouble. It would be best to stay away."

"But I know where the stuff you're looking for is, Pecos. I know a lot about the ranch."

I frowned. Andy had a point but it didn't make me happy. "We can talk about that, Andy. Things could get dangerous there real soon. I could use your help but I don't want you hurt."

"I won't get hurt, Pecos. I promise," he said still beaming.

"Boys your age think they will live forever and nothing will ever hurt them, until it does," Doc Burns told Andy in that calm way doctors have when they want to give good advice that their patient might not want to hear.

"We'll talk about that as well, Andy," I said. "Right now why don't you bring our horses around to the front? I want to say a few more things to Doc Burns and I'll be right down."

"Okay, Pecos, I'll go get them." He slammed the door in his haste and ran down the stairs, full of the boundless energy of youth. It was refreshing.

I turned back to the doctor. "He told me that Carter Brantley threatened to kill the people in the hotel if Esther Mallory didn't marry him when he comes back from wherever he went. Andy heard him say he'd be back in a week or less. I can't let him kill those people. I need to stop him somehow and cutting off the laudanum was the easiest and best chance I had to turn the odds in my favor. Now I need a new plan."

He sat down in front of his desk and pulled off the spectacles then rubbed his eyes with his finger and thumb. "I'm just a country sawbones now. Military plans aren't my strong suit."

"I can handle the military side of things, Doc, but I was hoping I could spare you the extra work of treating all the wounded men such action could produce. It seems if I can't simply cut off the supply of laudanum to these people maybe somehow we could switch it with something else. That way the effects of not having the opium would be the same yet no one would suspect that we'd tampered with the drug, at least not in time to stop my plan. The trouble I have is with slipping onto the ranch. As you told Andy, it will be dangerous."

He sat there in his chair and stared at me, eyes unfocused, seemingly lost in some thought hopefully spurred by what I'd said. Then he leaped to his feet, mumbling something that sounded like, "magnum cycle," over and over and rushed to a nearby bookshelf that also held a lot of rocks. He yanked down a large, leather bound volume and thumbed hurriedly through the pages.

I stood my ground and waited for his apparent fit of mania to subside; hoping whatever obsessed him would quickly come to fruition and produce a helpful outcome for me.

At last he seemed to have found what he sought. He

THE BETRAYED

lugged the heavy volume to his desk and sat in the chair once more. Then he hung the spectacles back over his ears, opened the book and using his forefinger as a guide quickly scanned the pages in front of him.

Then he scampered back to the shelf and pulled down a hefty rock that was almost white. He held it up and shook it at me. "Maybe this will solve your problem, Mr. Quinn. It's magnacite, a mineral that has been proven to cause diarrhea in people who take enough of it orally. I'll make a solution with it that will resemble laudanum and if you can slip into that adobe building you can switch the laudanum with the potion I make for you.

"I just gave Andy the business about how dangerous it is for him to slip onto that ranch. Now you want me to do it to put something you make from a rock into jugs of whiskey? Doctor, I think you must have rocks in your head."

"Captain, I didn't lug this chunk of God's bounty all the way out here from Pennsylvania for nothing. It's got some powerful qualities. It will give a man a bad case of the runs, similar to what happens when a man stops taking laudanum. The men on that ranch will most certainly get severe discomfort from my potion, and between the opium withdrawal of the cowboys and the magnesium salts in this white rock for the gunmen they could all be utterly helpless to resist you and your men when you take over the Bar D. Now are you game or do you have a better idea?"

He'd stumped me. At this point I had no clue what I

would do if we couldn't simply cut off the supply of laudanum and then move in after the men begin to suffer.

"This sounds complicated, Doc. They put the laudanum into the whiskey and they go through a lot of jugs every day. How can I get this rock into that whiskey out at the ranch?"

He pushed his glasses back up on his nose. "You don't understand, Quinn. I make a solution of the magnesium in the rock that I give orally to patients who have a blockage, well, back there. It looks a lot like laudanum though it tastes a different. Perhaps we could do that here? You could just carry some full jugs out there."

"They must go through ten or twenty jugs of whiskey a day, Doc. That's an awful lot."

"And they get a wagon load of whiskey every month."

"So all we need to do is switch out the laudanum with whatever it is you come up with."

"They must return the jugs that the whiskey comes in every time they take a load out there. There are empties downstairs right now. I've seen them just yesterday. If we fill them maybe we can switch them with the ones at the ranch."

"You mean maybe I can switch them, don't you Doc?"

He put the rock on his desktop. "Someone has to do it."

"The trouble is I can get killed doing it," I

complained. "Tell me Doc, if the cowboys at the ranch and the people at the hotel drink the same laudanum why can the cowboys work and the others are just wastrels."

"I understand from Murphy that the ranch hands weren't allowed to drink until after supper. The people in the hotel drink all day long. As far as I know that would be the difference."

"I guess that makes sense. Thanks Doc."

A rapid thumping came from the stairs outside. Then, before Doc Burns could get out of his chair, someone knocked loud at the door.

"It's Andy," I said. "I'll let him in." When I pulled open the door he rushed past me.

"Wow, it's pretty hot out there now, Pecos," he said. "The horses are waiting."

"All right, we'll go," I told him then turned to Burns. "Make up your potion, Doc. I'll see what I can do, but there's something missing that I need to understand in order for this to work."

"I'll count on you to do this, Captain."

"Don't count on any man until after he comes back from the fight."

"You'll get it done. I'm sure." He followed us to the door and closed it after we left.

Andy raced back down the steps and was in the saddle by the time I got to the ground. He looked over to me as he waited. "You and Doc are wondering about that shed where they keep the whiskey, I know. I went in there once. There are two shelves they keep it on and each one has a different jug on it. The shelves were near empty when I went in. One had jugs that were brown and the other almost white. I guess I'm not smart enough to know the difference."

Something in what he said caught me. Then my now reformed memory roared back. That first day, when I went into the saloon, Pete had offered me whiskey or liquor. I took the liquor. It came in a white jug and tasted funny. Later, when Ringo and his cronies came in they had whiskey. It was in a brown jug and tasted like cheap rotgut should. Could the white jug have the laudanum and could that be mixed right under the doctor's nose downstairs at the general store?

"Hang on here, Andy. You just might have solved my problem."

"I did? Holy smokes, I didn't know you had one," he joked happily.

"We'll see. Let's go in the store."

"Are we gonna get more stuff?" he asked, sounding on top of the world.

Inside Benson ran up at once, a worried expression on his face. "Is everything all right?"

"Actually, we are happy with the things we bought but it's just come to my attention that you deliver whiskey to the Bar D once a month. Is that correct?"

His mouth fell open wide and didn't seem to shut. He looked like he could swallow a fly. "I can't discuss the services I perform for Mr. Drake, sir," he finally said and somehow found a smile to add to his words.

"Look, Benson, I already know you do it so listen carefully to what I tell you. Doc Burns is going to give you something to add to those white jugs instead of the laudanum. It will help the folks there with the dyspepsia so many of them have. You'll get those jugs out to the ranch as soon as you are done, then bring all the brown ones you find there back here. Now that should be simple enough. You can add any extra costs you incur to Mr. Drake's bill."

"This is highly out of the ordinary, Mister. Did you say what your name is?"

"My name is Quinn. I'm a captain under the colonel's command. He's away for a few days and this is a serious situation. We need your cooperation a great deal. I'm positive the Colonel will appreciate you for your help with the men who are ailing."

He looked at me warily. I was not a familiar face and that appeared to bother him.

"Hey Mister," Andy called to him. "There are sure a lot of sick folks on the ranch. If you don't help out Mr. Drake's gonna be real mad at you. He don't like folks who won't help."

The boy's comments seemed to make Benson flustered. Sweat popped from the top of his bald head and he mopped it quickly with his hand which he then wiped on his trousers. I was sure he didn't want to go against the wishes of Brantley, his biggest customer, but what I'd asked him to do wasn't anything like what Brantley ever had and he didn't know me from Adam.

Still, I could sense he was almost convinced. "The

boy makes a good point, Mr. Benson. Drake will be not be pleased if you don't help him out with this, but on the other hand—"

"No, no, I'll do what Mr. Drake wants," he said real fast. "After all, how could adding a medicine that Doc Burns made to the whiskey for the ranch possibly hurt anyone?"

"That's fine, Mr. Benson. I'll make sure to tell Mr. Drake how cooperative you've been."

As Andy and I turned to leave Benson followed us to the door. "If Doc Burns can get me what I need today I'll have that stuff out to the ranch the day after tomorrow," he said. "Mr. Drake can count on Tom Benson. You can bet your bottom dollar on that."

"I'll let the doctor know," I told him as we walked out into the heat.

Andy looked up to me. "Do you want me to tell the doc real fast, Pecos?"

"You bet, and then we'll get out of here."

Andy raced up the steps once more, the door opened before he got to the top and I heard him explain how Benson would take the new whiskey out to the ranch the day after tomorrow if the doctor could get the medicine down to him today.

Burns stepped out onto the stair landing. He looked down at me and nodded. "Yes, I'll get that medication to Benson just as soon as I can. It's very important that those men have it quickly," he told me in a voice that I was sure the store keeper could hear easily if he was listening, and I'd bet a new twenty-dollar gold double eagle he was.

I tipped my hat to him. "I appreciate it, Doc." And with that I rode off toward the ranch. Andy took the hint and came with me. When we were well out of sight of the store I stopped.

"You were a real trooper back there, Andy. Your story about Drake being mad pushed Benson over the edge. What made you think of it?"

He laughed. "It wasn't hard. Mr. Brantley's always mad about something."

"How do you know about the opium in the whiskey?"

He glanced at me with a cockeyed look on his face. "What's opium?"

"The Doc calls it laudanum. It's a drug that makes people act like the folks in the hotel."

"Oh," he muttered under his breath. "Esther always said she thought there was something in the whiskey they drank but she didn't know what it was. They drink it all day long."

"A lot of the cow hands at the ranch drink it too, but Brantley only lets them drink it after supper. Hopefully when Benson does what we asked him to do then all those men will get sick for a while. That's when we can take the ranch. Brantley's gone, and so is Ringo and the gun hands. I hope there will only be a few men left who are able to resist."

"What are you going to do when Mr. Brantley and Ringo come back?"

"I have something in mind, Andy, but it's always best to keep future plans secret. You could still be captured by the enemy, you know."

"I ain't gonna be captured, Pecos."

Now I laughed. "I hope not. You're too important."

He grinned real big. "There's a back way onto the ranch, you know?"

That hit me like a bolt out of the blue. "I thought there were only two routes into that valley, the one off the trail that's up ahead and the one from your camp."

"There's a third way from the back side," he said with a wide boyish grin.

"I always assumed the ranch backed up on the Pecos River."

"That's the Pecos River?" he yelled. "I thought that it was way down south."

"It's a long river, Andy."

"So Esther used to live on this same river then?" he asked.

"You bet she did. So did I, and Paine Dodd and probably some others in that hotel."

"Holy smokes," he muttered.

"Why don't you show me this back door to Brantley's ranch?"

"What if I get captured doing it?" he replied, sounding almost defiant now.

"Then it's a good thing I didn't tell you my plans for dealing with Brantley and Ringo."

His grin came back in all its glory. "We need to follow the rocks on this side of the ranch to the east but we can't get close. There are some gullies that run out of them. We can ride in the biggest one. That's the secret to getting to the river easy."

"Lead the way, son."

We pulled off the trail well before the rocks that encircled the Bar D ranch and headed east. Soon we came to one of the gullies. I could see how rain had run from the rocks during the fierce storms that occasionally came to this usually dry place. That water had carved gashes in the land as it rushed toward the Pecos River.

Andy pointed to it. "We'll ride into that wash here while it's still shallow," he said.

Soon another gully ran into the one we now rode in and it grew deeper. A little further along another one came in and the gully grew bigger again. Several more times this happened and I realized that in a bad storm this now dry gully could quickly become a raging torrent. Without thinking I peered all around the sky looking for a dark rain cloud. There were none.

Then a flock of ducks flew over us likely headed to the water. The gully had gotten so deep the top was above our heads. As we neared the river I could hear it rushing downstream.

The brown, muddy Pecos had carved a deep path for itself through the dry sandy ground. The water was filled with so much soil and dirt that I doubted if it was fit to drink. The river ran slowly on to Texas many days ride south of here.

The level of the water however was lower than the

sides of the channel that the Pecos now meandered through. We turned to ride alongside the stream and found ourselves on a narrow sandy beach. Soon Andy turned up another small, dry gully that also dumped rain water into the river. It rose quickly to a notch in the rocks that I realized went all the way through to the ranch.

"Hold up, Andy," I told him. "You've been an adventurous boy. This could be very helpful to me, but I wonder why there is no one watching back here."

"You mean like guards?" he asked.

"Yes, exactly."

"Shucks, Pecos, I don't know. I've come here a lot and I've never seen anybody."

"You've been all the way through the rocks?"

"You bet. I've been to the barn lots and gotten close to the ranch house. The stream we saw that night you stayed at my camp runs into the river down a little way. All the cows drink from that stream up on the ranch. The water is a lot cleaner there. The men go with the cows."

I had to grin at him. He was proving to be a valuable and fun companion. "That makes sense. Let's go to the rocks and scout around a bit."

We rode real slow and I scanned for any Bar D men often with my field glasses. On this side of the rocks we stopped and I took a long look. I don't see any sign of a cow or a man."

"You can see the ranch house and the barn pretty easy from up on the rocks," Andy said.

I looked where he pointed. "Hold my horse and I'll go up there." I gave him the reins and was soon scampering up to the top. Andy was right. Even without the binoculars I could see the layout of the spread easily. The ranch house was off to the left where the ring of boulders curved back to mark the dividing line with Brantleyville. Farther to the right sat a large barn made like the one at Miles Durant's place, with a sod roof and sides of pine limbs that were open enough to let the air circulate inside. The adobe shack where the booze was kept stood closer to me.

Between them were a group of three smaller adobe buildings, each half sunk in the earth and covered with a sod roof. I'd missed them with the first sweep of the binoculars. They were most likely bunk houses for the men with a common cook house in the middle. The cow hands who got the laudanum laced whiskey would sleep closest to the adobe shed behind the barn, and the gunmen who got their whiskey straight would get their shuteye nearer to the ranch house.

The whole scene was a bit much for me to take. All this had happened since the end of the war. Most of that time I'd spent working for the Union horse soldiers scouting out Comanche so the Yankee cavalry could send them to their happy hunting ground or wherever a Comanche went after a bullet from a Springfield blew a hole through him. But the Yankees had learned well during the war and had pretty much pushed the Comanche onto the reservation in the Indian Territory by now. My job as a scout was done, but as of today I had Colonel Carter Brantley to scout, and soon I would personally see to it that he is sent to his own private happy hunting ground with help from a few old soldiers and one brave boy.

I put the field glasses back to my eyes and scanned the terrain again. Riders on the far side of the barn moved through a large number of cattle that grazed among the mesquite and sage. The cows nearest the ranch house drank from the fresh water streams that flowed towards the Pecos to my left. It looked like a peaceful, well hidden, cattle operation. Whatever reason the Colonel had for a shipment of Winchester repeating rifles didn't fit with this pastoral scene.

A thin plume of smoke rose from the direction of Miles Durant's ranch. It likely came from his cook house. I'd seen enough. After the play-acting Andy and I had done at Benson's store I thought it best not to ride by the place again until the whiskey had been delivered here to the Bar D, and I fully intended to return to make sure that happened. But for now we would follow the smoke north through the prairie. I put the field glasses away and scampered back to where Andy waited.

He greeted me with a heartwarming but completely smug grin that told me right off he knew a lot more about this ranch than I ever though a boy his age would. We rode back to the muddy Pecos River and then back up the gully. When we came out onto the prairie, we headed across the flat hard ground.

"Where're we going, Pecos."

"Back to Miles Durant's place, but I don't want Benson to see us ride by his store heading north. He might get second thoughts and that would screw up our plans."

"You mean he wouldn't deliver Doc Burns' medicine?"

"You bet and you and I need to come back to the ranch to see if that wagon shows up with the new whiskey mixed with Doc Burns' medicine."

"Yeah, that's great," he yelled.

That comment had gotten his spirits up at once. Andy sure liked to sneak around Brantley's ranch. I thought back to my childhood, a period in my life I still had no problem recalling, and realized I'd been that way too. My brother and I spent an awful lot of time peeking through a side window at the Longhorn Saloon in Houston just to figure out what went on in a place our sweet, God fearing mother hated so badly and railed about constantly.

"How long have you had Willow, Andy?" I asked partly to get his mind off what we needed to do at the ranch and the gun play that could be involved. It was also something that had been a burr under my saddle for a while. No one else at Brantleyville had a horse.

"I got her at the same time I started living up by the spring where I met you."

"Didn't the Colonel get upset about you having a horse?"

"He didn't like it none, but Esther put her foot down for me. I couldn't stay at the spring without a horse to ride into town on and she knew I was bound and determined to get out of that place any way I could. Brantley said I could have Willow but only if I didn't take her to town in the daylight. Esther wasn't so happy with that but it suited me fine. I didn't want to be there when the hotel people were in the diner anymore."

"I don't blame you for that. Where did you get her?"

"She belonged to a saddle tramp. I guess she ran off after Ringo shot the guy. When she wound up at Esther's place I hid her in the shed for a few days and we got to be pretty good friends. I'd feed her and all and then we'd go for a ride after dark. Brantley caught me when he came in to see Esther. Right then and there they had a knockdown, drag out hullabaloo over Willow. Esther told him either I get Willow or she'd take me and leave Brantleyville."

"Esther seems to be the only person who can get her way with the Colonel," I said but I felt sure she wouldn't leave the people at the hotel behind. It wasn't in her nature. Did Colonel Brantley not know that?

We rode down into another small dry wash from the run off between small rises and quickly came up the other side. The thin column of gray smoke from the cook fire at Miles Durant's place pierced the blue sky ahead as we continued across the sage covered prairie.

"Pecos," Andy called a cautious way. "You don't like Mr. Brantley much I know, but I been wondering if you really did come here to shoot him like those saddle tramps wanted to."

I stopped my horse and looked over to him. "I like Brantley a lot less now than I did when I got here, Andy, but I don't want to shoot him. Still, he's caused plenty of suffering for a lot of people. He'll have to pay for that."

"He can afford it. He's the only fellow I know that has any money."

"I guess he would be. No one in Brantleyville has any. That's part of the problem. It looks like he had a lot of folks killed down south. Then he stole their cattle. That's two serious crimes. The Yankee's would hang him."

"That trouble down south, on the Pecos, that's what started all this ain't it."

"It sure is. You were there. I heard you'd been away with Esther that day but you two got there after the killing happened."

"That's what she told me too. I don't remember much about it."

"I don't remember a lot of it either. I got shot. That's why I came here but it looks like the story Brantley told wasn't true. There were no Comanche who raided our homesteads and the Yankee Cavalry wasn't hot on our tail. It looks like Ringo and some of his men killed my family and Esther's husband as well as a lot of other good people."

"Then Ringo should hang too," he added.

"Yep, Ringo and the men who were with him, but

they're responsible for killing a lot more men since then. You know that. Ringo shot the man who once owned Willow."

He sat on his horse and stared at the ground. "Sometimes, when Paine Dodd and Esther are talking and there's nobody else around, I hear him tell her that Brantley and Ringo should hang, just like you said. He always seems different when there's no one but Esther there. I guess maybe you're right, but I'm really not sure what it means to hang Brantley."

I stopped my horse once more. It hit me for the first time how isolated from the world Andy really had been. Now I would have to explain to him what it meant to hang a man.

"There are good folks and bad folks, Andy, and we have a government that sets laws people have to abide by to live with each other. Two of the worst things any man can do are to steal the property of another person or to kill them. When they are accused of either of those crimes they have a trial where they get a chance to prove they didn't do anything wrong while the people want to show they did something very bad. A jury of twelve honest citizens has to decide if they are guilty or not guilty."

Andy had stopped Willow too and was listening to every word I said. The idea that some men were criminals and could be punished for their crime was clearly new to him.

"Men guilty of killing are hanged," I went on. "A rope is put around their neck and they're dropped several feet. The rope stops their fall and snaps their neck. That kills them."

"Then you think Mr. Brantley should be hanged?" he asked sounding confused.

"I think he should have a trial and if he's found guilty then he should hang."

"But you think he's guilty don't you."

"It sure looks that way." I gave the sorrel a nudge and we rode on.

He was quiet for quite a while as we trotted among the sage, picking our path carefully to stay on the open ground. "Pecos," he called to me, "does that mean Ringo should hang too."

"Ringo was wanted by the Yankees before he started riding with Brantley. He's killed a lot of men since, including the settlers down south on the Pecos and those men who came here looking for Brantley. They were just like me. They didn't know what happened. They just knew something was wrong and Brantley was their commander. He was responsible."

"For Esther's husband too?"

"He sure was."

"Did Ringo actually kill him then?"

"Probably, either Ringo or one of his men."

"Then will they have a trial and get hanged?'

"I don't know, Andy. I expect both of them would rather die fighting than face a trial. They know they're guilty. They'll have us out gunned, plus they have more men than we do. We'll have to surprise them and that will be difficult, but if we catch them they might hang."

"Does Esther know about Mr. Brantley?" Andy wondered.

"I think she does."

"Then why would she marry him?"

"I can't say for sure, son, but it could be that she has no choice."

We rode on and again Andy was quiet. I knew that the things he'd learned about the evil deeds of Colonel Brantley had an effect on him. They'd certainly had a profound one on me. The question was how he would handle them, and, for that matter, how would I handle them?

I could see Miles Durant's ranch house now and the barn with the bunk house and cook house off to the side. We were almost back. The ride across the prairie had been a little rougher than the trail I'd followed when I came up from Texas but wasn't that bad. I knew I could take a group of armed men back that way when the time came. Now my mind switched to the cook house fire that made the smoke we followed. I was getting hungry.

Then Andy pulled Willow to a stop. "Pecos, if Colonel Brantley has better guns and more men than you do then you might lose and Esther would have to marry him, right?"

I nodded, "Yep, that's about it."

"Well I can't help you with more men but there's a lot of repeating rifles on the ranch."

"Really," I said, "and I suppose you know exactly where they are?"

"They're in the same place where the whiskey is. I guess so they can get to them easy."

"Can we go there tomorrow?"

"Sure, we can do that."

"Those guns will help us when Brantley gets back. Now let's see if we can get a meal."

"I'm hungry too, but I got to tell you there are two big guns on wagon wheels there."

"Wheels! They must be field guns. Andy, are you sure?"

"Yes sir. I saw them a few days ago. They're in the barn hooked up to other stuff."

It sounded like both the limbers and caissons were still with the guns. Hopefully with full ammunition boxes atop each. I had to know. "How much do you go onto that ranch, Andy?"

"Brantley comes to see Esther two or three times a week. I don't like to see her when he's there so I go out to the ranch."

I shook my head at his honest confession. "Can we get into the barn at night?"

"I've done it lots of times. That's how I get oats for Willow," he said with a big grin.

"Do you know where those big guns came from?" I wondered.

"No sir, but I didn't see them in the barn until the middle of winter."

"You go into the barn real regular, don't you?"

"Willow likes her oats so I guess I gotta."

"If those really are field guns with ammunition Willow might get all the oats she wants."

He patted the neck of his horse. "Did you hear that, Willow? Pecos likes you too."

"We'll pack some food and wait till things quiet down then we'll go inside the barn and check those guns. If Benson gets the whiskey there day after tomorrow it'll be our only chance."

"Why's that, Pecos?" he asked.

"The gunmen won't feel like fighting after they drink Doc Burns new potion."

11

ANDY AND I RODE OUT FROM MILES DURANT'S RANCH the next day. The sun hung low in the clear western sky and we followed the route we'd taken coming here the day before. I'd packed dried beef and a dozen biscuits just in case we needed them. Andy had several cans of peaches and a few apples. We'd be at Brantley's ranch into the evening. It could be a long night.

I'd explained my plan for taking the ranch to Miles. He backed me all the way. He would get the men together and start preparing them to take the Bar D. Andy and I would spend most of tomorrow watching to see if the whiskey from Benson's store really showed up. If it did we would raid the ranch early the next morning. I hadn't told Andy. In fact the only ones who knew were Miles Durant and me. The less people to whom I told my plans the better our secrecy. If the men at the Bar D found out our attack could be quashed quickly.

Andy had been quiet ever since we started out. I knew he was looking forward to coming along with me. He always seemed to have a great time and for a boy his age this had to be exciting. For some reason he seemed out of sorts.

"Why so quiet, Andy," I asked him.

"I don't know, Pecos. I'm worried I guess."

"We're doing something dangerous. A little worry is normal."

"Oh, I'm not so much worried about us. It's Esther that eats at me."

"What did Esther do?"

"Oh, she ain't done anything, but when Mr. Benson cuts off that laudanum stuff the people at the hotel are going to start acting real strange and they're going to need a lot more attention from her. She could get hurt then. I don't want that."

"You like Esther a lot, don't you?"

"Shucks, sure I do. That's why I'm so out of sorts today."

"I worry about her too," I told him in as calm a voice as I could muster.

His head jerked around. His eyes bored into mine. "You like Esther, don't you?"

I stopped the sorrel and returned his glare. "She's a good woman," I told him. "She doesn't deserve to live like she does. She'll marry Brantley if it's the only way she can keep those people alive."

"You want to marry her, I know you do."

It struck me that he sounded more like a jealous

suitor than an adopted son. "Brantley's the one who's asking her to marry him, Andy. Is that why you're mad at him?"

"Yeah, I reckon it is," he said in a little calmer tone. "But after that I got to thinking that the only reason why you wanted to stop Mr. Brantley is so you could marry Esther yourself. Is that it? Do you want to marry her?" He sounded mad again.

"Hey, hold your horses there. I've been living mostly in the wilderness of Texas for the last five years. I'm coarse and crude and probably will scare the living daylights out of any descent woman and that includes Esther Mallory. If I asked her she'd show me the door before I could get off my knees."

"Well I think she likes you an awful lot—"

"And you're worried I'll take her away from you," I barked back at him.

"If she marries Brantley I'll never be able to see her anymore, so why would things be different if she marries you?" he yelled.

"Maybe because I'm not Brantley," I told him patiently.

He had to think about that a while. We rode on through the sage.

Finally he looked my way. "If it's twixt you and Brantley I'd pick you, Pecos, but I sure would like things to go back to how they used to be."

"A lot of us here would like for things to be like they once were, but that can never happen. They say that time marches on and when it does things change. You need to look at what we're about to do from the bright side. For the first time since the war ended all the folks in Brantleyville can be free of the chains that hold them there under the Colonel's thumb."

"Am I still under that thumb?" he asked with a sad tone to his words.

"In some ways, yes you are," I said gently. "But on the other hand you're starting to stretch your legs. When you got Willow and left Esther's place why didn't you keep riding?"

He looked at me with gloomy eyes. "I don't know, I guess I didn't want to leave her."

"Maybe you weren't ready to leave her."

He pondered on that for a while. "Ringo killed more saddle tramps and I got one of those horses. I tried to get Esther to leave with me, but she wouldn't go. She said it didn't matter anyway, Brantley would find us before we could get very far."

"She was right, you know. He would have found you."

His face turned sad again. "I know," was all he said.

Soon we came to the gully that would lead us to the river. We turned left and rode down the center of it until we came to the muddy flow of the Pecos. Then we edged along the narrow beach and headed to the gap in the rocks where we went inland.

We hadn't gotten far when Andy stopped his horse. "Do you know Blackie, Pecos? He's the fellow who bosses the men who watch Mr. Brantley's cows."

"Would he be the guy in the long black beard?"

"He sure would."

"We met when Murphy broke his leg. I wanted to help him and Blackie got mad. Like Ringo he tried to pull a gun on me. I talked him into letting me take Murphy to Doc Burns."

"I heard him tell his men to shoot you on sight anytime they find you. He says the orders came straight from Mr. Brantley."

"I'm not surprised, Andy. Blackie wanted to shoot me when we met. I got the drop on him and that slowed him down some, but when did you hear that and where were you?"

"Remember the night when I saw you at Esther's and she wanted me to go with you?"

"Well, sure."

"I'd just come back from the ranch. I was listening outside the guards' bunkhouse. They were drinking and Blackie was talking loud and sounding mean. That's when I left."

I stared at him. It bothered me that he's been lurking around Brantley's ranch like he did but he'd come up with a lot of good information that I knew I would use soon, but something else ate at me about the story he just told me.

"If you were at the ranch that night how did you get to Esther's place so fast? It would take you hours to go all the way around."

He looked at me with that playful smile he sometimes had. "There's a back way to Esther's place just like there's one here. I just rode down the river and went through the rocks."

"You are full of surprises, Andy. But I don't want you to come back here to the ranch alone anymore. Things have gotten too dangerous."

"Blackie or Ringo won't hurt me," he said. "Esther would be mad as all get out."

"Brantley is threatening to kill a lot of people if she doesn't marry him. I don't think you're safe at all. He's ruthless. He'll do what he must to get his way. Mind what I say, please."

He thought about it for a bit then looked up. "I can still come here with you can't I?"

"If we can take over this ranch and catch the Colonel you can come here anytime."

"But it won't be so much fun then."

"You don't know that for sure, do you? It just might be more fun."

He gave me a look that held both doubt in what I'd said but also carried a hope that maybe I could be right. I'd felt that way so many times as a boy when my dad suggested similar things to me. Now I can look back and see how he was always right. Then I realized I hadn't thought about my father in many years. It was a good memory and I welcomed it with a smile.

Andy's chin rose as his chest swelled proudly. "Yeah but I like the excitement. It won't be as much fun if I know I can't get caught."

"If anyone here knows you're helping me like you are right now they won't hesitate to get rid of you in spite of what Esther might do. More than likely you'll just disappear and Esther and anyone else in Brantleyville who cares will never know what happened."

This time I saw the shock that flashed across his face. What I'd said hit him in the gut like he'd been rammed by a bull. "I never thought of that," he mumbled.

"Well, now you know. Keep it in mind."

We rode into the rocks just as the last twilight faded away. Across the vast open sky stars began to pop out everywhere. Andy led me onto a rocky trail along the edge of the notch that outlined the path we would take into the ranch later tonight. We left the horses where they couldn't be seen easily by anyone who might come by here. Then we climbed the tallest rock.

There, from our vantage point above the spread, we could see lights from all the buildings except the barn which stood out as a large dark shadow beyond the bunk houses. We waited until at last the lamps went out, first in the adobe where the whiskey, guns and ammunition were kept and then, at last, in the bunkhouses.

Andy poked me. "See the torches," he said.

I saw the small flickering lights easily as they moved around the ranch. "I see them."

"They always stay near the ranch house and in front of the buildings. That's why it's easy to get in from back here," Andy told me and from what I saw he was right.

"Are you ready?" I asked him.

"You bet I am."

We climbed down carefully then made our way through the notch and onto the ranch. Andy led me beside the bunkhouse with the gunmen in it and then across to the barn.

"In here," he whispered.

I slipped in a slightly open barn door behind him. Inside it was almost totally dark. I could hardly see at all. I felt Andy's hand pulling on my shirt sleeve. "This way," he whispered.

He towed me off to the right. Soon he stopped me, took my hand and put it on a cold metal tube, a cannon barrel without a doubt. I felt the muzzle then eased down the gun until the carriage stopped me. I headed around a wheel until I came to the limber behind the gun. I felt around for the ammunition box and opened it. It was full with canister rounds right on top. Andy pulled me to the caisson. It had two ammunition boxes, both full. I'd found what I wanted to.

"Let's go, Andy," I whispered. He tugged on my shirt again and we headed toward the barn door that still stood slightly ajar. I could see a little bit of light that leaked in from the stars.

Just then I heard footsteps outside. "Hey, Max, the barn door's open."

The voice was close, way too close for my comfort.

"What do you want to do, look for a stray horse?"

"If Blackie sees that door he'll have a fit."

"I'm beat. It's been a long day. Let's get some whiskey."

"Yeah, I'm ready. No horse will go through that crack anyhow."

Their footsteps faded. I sucked in a deep breath. We'd had a close call. Andy tugged on my sleeve again. We slipped out the door and hurried back toward our mounts.

We hadn't gone far when a familiar voice broke the silence. "Damn you, Max. You know what the boss says about barn doors open at night. Shut that door now."

"Aw, Blackie, them animals ain't going nowhere."

"It ain't the horses the boss is worried about. It's that Quinn fellow and the damn boy, if you see 'em shoot 'em, kill 'em. You'll make Brantley real glad. Now close that damn door."

"Yes sir, Blackie. Right away."

Andy and I were out in the open and only covered by the darkness. I put my hand on his shoulder and pushed him down. He got the hint real fast and in no time we were flat on the ground while Max and his buddy trudged back to the barn. Then I heard the creak of the big door closing and the clatter of the wooden latch they threw down to keep the animals in. It would have kept us in too if we hadn't gotten out when we did.

"That damn Blackie's too bloodthirsty. I like that boy. I won't kill him," Max said.

"If you don't Blackie's liable to kill you."

"Yeah, he's killed a few good men here. I don't think I want to shoot Captain Quinn either. He was a pretty good officer back in the war. He really cared about his men."

"You aren't working for Quinn any more, Boyd. You're working for Blackie."

"Yeah, but there's more here who feel like I do. Most won't speak out though."

"I can't say you're wrong. I just hope I don't come face to face with Quinn or the boy."

Their voices faded as they headed off to the bunkhouse. I kept my hand on Andy. I didn't want him jumping up too soon. Meanwhile I listened as carefully as I could for more footsteps of men heading this way for their nightly allotment of whiskey.

After a while I whispered to the boy, "Let's go, real quiet."

We slowly stood then eased off toward the river. I still listened hard for any sound of one of Brantley's men but the farther we got from the barn the safer I felt. At last we made it to our horses, mounted and soon rode through the rocks and stopped by the river.

"That was close, Andy. If those two men had locked us in the barn we would be in trouble. You heard what they said about you. Do you still think Brantley's men won't hurt you?"

"I heard him, Pecos. He scared me near out of my skin. I always figured that if I got killed Esther would give Brantley the business. I guess I was wrong."

"I doubt she would ever know what happened to you. You would simply disappear."

"You told me the truth, Pecos. You always do that,"

he said in a shaky voice. "Thanks," he added sounding a little more sure of himself.

"It's good to have friends you can trust, Andy. I hope you trust me."

"Except for Esther you're the only friend I have, Pecos."

It hit me right off how strange that sounded coming from a thirteen year old boy. "I'm sure that soon you'll find plenty more friends, son."

"I never figured much on having friends, not in Brantleyville."

"If we can take this ranch while Ringo and his men are off somewhere with Brantley, we can make a new life for you and me both. I need that as much as you do."

"I never thought of that. Wasn't chasing Comanche pretty fun?"

"Chasing Comanche is dangerous. I'm lucky to be here."

"I'm lucky you're here too," he said and sounded a lot more optimistic now.

"We didn't get a look at those repeating rifles so we have a little more time tonight. How about we go see Esther real fast then check on Doc Burns on our way back to Miles' spread?"

"Yeah, I'd like that. We can go in through the back the way I told you about."

"After you, my friend," I said and we headed south on the narrow beach beside the river.

We crossed the creek that ran from the ranch and

came to another dry gully that took rain water from the line of rocks down to the Pecos, but now, in the dim light of evening, those rocks looked like an unbroken ridge. Still Andy turned up it. Soon we came to the first large crag rising some forty or fifty feet on our left and on the far side of it the gully turned south in front of an equally big rock that from the river had looked to be a part of a solid line blocking the valley. Then we turned right alongside that boulder. We passed it and climbed to the valley floor.

The tiny town of Brantleyville stood clear in the moonlight a short distance away. I could see now how Andy had been able to get between the town and the ranch so quickly. In only one year after he got Willow he'd managed to explore both locations in ways none of the men from the Bar D ever had. I felt a great deal of pride in what he'd done.

The saloon was dark as we rode by. Across the dusty street no lamps burned in the hotel, but light still shone from the windows in the back of the diner. Esther was awake.

"She's waiting for me," Andy said just as I'd been thinking the same thing.

We left the horses in back and he raced into the kitchen. "Hi Esther," he called.

"Andy, you have new clothes. You look so good. Is Paul with you," she asked.

"If you mean Pecos he's outside."

"I've been so worried about you both. I don't know what you're up to," she said.

I could hear the tension in her words. I understood her concern for the boy, especially after what we'd heard earlier near the barn, but did she worry about me too? It sounded like it.

Then the door opened and she rushed out and threw her arms around me. "Oh, Paul, I'm so glad you're safe," she said softly into my ear.

I couldn't help myself. I kissed her.

Then Andy stepped onto the porch. "I told you she liked you, Pecos."

Esther pulled away from me and turned. "I do like Paul very much, Andy, but that doesn't mean I love you any less."

"Well, I like him too. He's going to help us—"

"Don't say too much, Andy. You never know when someone else might be listening."

"Yeah, I guess you're right. Max and Boyd didn't know we were there," he went on and I knew he was talking about how they said Blackie had told them to kill him on sight. He hadn't mentioned it on the way over here but it must be eating at his insides something fierce.

"That might be a little too much too, Andy. Let's all go inside."

"What happened tonight, Paul," Esther whispered to me as we went into the kitchen. She wanted to know what we did and I didn't blame her.

Andy sat at the table and Esther headed to the stove. "Are you hungry?" she asked. "I have some fried chicken and fresh bread, and there's coffee too."

"I love fried chicken," Andy told her. "We have stuff to eat in our bags but it'll keep."

Esther looked at me and I nodded then sat next to him. She poured us both coffee then put bread and butter on the table. Andy dug right in, cutting himself a thick slice and piling butter on it. Esther filled two plates with chicken and potatoes and put them in front of us.

"We're going to cut off the laudanum in the whiskey the folks at the hotel get." I told her.

"Is that what causes their problems?"

"It is. They'll get real sick. It'll last a week maybe. We don't know for sure. At the same time we're going to take the ranch from Brantley's men. If we can do that then we'll be in good shape when he returns with Ringo and most of his gunmen. I'm afraid this will put a big strain on you. I'll try to get a few men here to help."

"Paine Dodd doesn't drink the whiskey. He will help," she said.

"Are you sure?"

"Yes, we talk a lot when no one is around. He's very angry at Brantley but he will help if he has too."

"Good, I think you'll need him, but honestly I have no idea what will happen. They most likely will not be able to sleep. They'll have to go to the outhouse a lot. They may be restless and agitated. I expect they'll drink all the whiskey they can find in the hope it can help. I'd leave Andy with you but I'm afraid if any Brantley men come by here he could be hurt. I wonder, do you know Doc Burns?"

She seemed lost, even confused. "Is he a real doctor?" she wondered.

"Yes, he lives over the general store north of Brantley's ranch."

"I had no idea there was a doctor, or anyone else, anywhere near here."

"Andy and I will go by his place after we leave here and tell him what to expect. I want to take the ranch soon, while Brantley and his gunmen are away. I have a good plan but none of us have done anything like this since the war. I'll try to get the doctor to stop by here but his hands may be full if a lot of men are hurt. Still I'll send someone to you as soon as I can."

"And if it doesn't work?" she asked with a worried expression clouding her face.

"You may have a lot of wounded men to take care of."

"Oh, Paul, isn't there any other way?"

"I have high hopes, Esther, but even when we succeed in getting the ranch the real fight will come when Brantley returns. Hopefully some men at the ranch now will help us then."

"You mean they will fight Carter Brantley when he comes back?" she wondered.

"Some of them served in my troop. I believe they trust me but I also think there must be unrest among the hands on the ranch. A number of them have left already and they will be the ones who help take the Bar D. They have many friends still there."

Her face held a questioning look. "You said the Bar D. Is that the ranch?"

Brantley calls himself Drake now, at least to the doctor and a man named Benson who runs the general store up the road. Colonel Brantley is an outlaw, still wanted by the Yankees. He never surrendered the Thirty-ninth Texas and they will hold it against him."

"Why doesn't the Yankee Army take care of him? Can't you tell them where he is?"

"They don't have enough men to deal with all the Indians out here. As long as Colonel Brantley doesn't cause too much trouble they won't be bothered. We have no choice."

She looked to the boy, her concern clear. "What will happen to Andy?"

His head jerked up from the pile of chicken bones on his plate. His eyes darted from me to her. "I'm sticking with Pecos," he assured her.

I saw her face fall. That wasn't what she wanted to hear. "Esther, as hard as it might be for you to accept, staying with me might be the safest place for him to be," I said. "He's shared a lot of valuable information that led directly to what we are going to do. If things work out well then nothing will happen to either of us."

"And if things don't go well?" she asked her face still a gloomy mask.

"Things aren't going well for any of us right now. What we have is a Hobson's choice, either we accept what our lives have become or we try to improve our situation the best way we can. If it doesn't work out then we can't be that much worse off."

"Who's that Hobson guy, Pecos? Does he work for the Colonel," Andy wondered.

Esther broke a smile at what he said. "No, Andy. It's just an expression. It means take it or leave it and I guess Paul is right. Even if we fail to free ourselves from the yoke Brantley has forced on all of us we'll be no worse off than before."

"Is that why the folks at the hotel are so different from the guys at Miles Durant's spread, cause of this yoke thing Mr. Brantley forced on them?" Andy asked and looked confused.

"I think you pretty well understand it, Andy. Anything you don't get I'll explain on the way to Doc's place. We need to get moving." I stood, wiped my hands on my napkin and dropped it beside my empty plate. "The supper was first class, Esther. I enjoyed it a great deal. Andy and I will be back as soon as we can. You can expect folks at the hotel to start showing signs they're getting sick starting early day after tomorrow. They'll be in bad shape by nightfall."

She hurried over and threw her arms around me again. "Please take care of yourself, Paul, and watch out after Andy too. I'll worry about you both terribly."

I pulled her close and kissed her. When I let her go she went straight to the boy and hugged him tight. "You be careful, Andy. I want you to do everything Paul tells you. He knows best and when this is done I want to see you as soon as possible." She pulled back from him but left her hands on his shoulders. "Promise me, Andy."

"I promise, but don't worry so much. Pecos and me will be just fine."

She shook her head. "I wish I could believe that." She looked from the boy to me.

"Pray that things work out as I planned," I said. "We all deserve it."

"I hope you're right, Paul. I will pray my heart out."

"Let's go, Andy," I told him and soon we were riding away from the diner and heading toward the gap in the rocks near where I first saw him.

"I told you she liked you a lot, Pecos," he said in a low voice.

"I like her too, Andy, and I also like you just as she does."

"Yeah, I guess you're right about that. She sure seemed worried about me."

"I'm worried too, Andy. I'm glad you didn't tell her what we'd been doing or about the things we overheard at the ranch from Max and Boyd. That showed good sense on your part. It gives me a lot more reason to worry less about you."

"I guess what Max and Boyd said about Blackie wanting me killed did scare me some but I decided it was just talk. Why would he want me killed?"

"Maybe they think you know too much about the ranch. Maybe you've been seen sneaking around there more than you know."

"Gee, Pecos, do you believe that?"

"I think so, Andy, and until this is over I don't want you out of my sight unless I tell you. You are now my right hand man, understand?"

I looked over to see a huge grin on his face. I'd just chewed him out, or so I thought, and now he was happy. "What are you smiling about?" I had to ask.

"I'm your right hand man. That sounds pretty important."

"And that's where I want you at all times. You never know when I might need you again and when that time comes I want you close. I don't want you going anywhere alone, on the ranch or off it. Do you understand?"

"Oh, you didn't really believe what we heard from Max and Boyd, that Blackie wanted me killed, did you?" he said in a way that sounded like he still thought it was a joke.

"Yes, I believed every word and you certainly should. Blackie is a killer. Your life isn't worth a Mexican peso to him. He would love to shoot you. Stay with me, is that clear?"

He turned away and I got the feeling he was pouting. He'd done it before.

"Andy, Esther and I both love you very much. I hope to take that ranch with a minimum of shooting but if something goes wrong it could become a battle with shots coming from all around. It will be very dangerous for anyone there. Personally I would rather leave you at Miles Durant's place but I don't think you'll stay there and you might have a lot of knowledge about the ranch that you may not have told me. I could need you if things get out of hand."

He still didn't say anything for a while. I left him to his thoughts and we rode on.

"Pecos," he said finally. "I think you need me now."

I wondered if he was still sulking. "You're a big help to me Andy. I hope you know that." "There's somebody on the hill where I met you."

"You mean they're guarding the way into the valley like you once did," I asked, surprised he'd even noticed someone there in the dark at this distance.

"Do you think they're waiting for me?" he asked. His voice shivered. Was he finally afraid that Max and Boyd had been right and Blackie wanted him dead?

"I don't see them," I said. "Are you sure?"

"Yep, there are two of them sitting on the rock. They move around and something flashes in the moonlight. There it goes now."

I caught the motion Andy saw. I held my eyes on the spot and pulled up my field glasses. I could see them now, two men, like he'd said, sitting high on the rock and looking along the trail as it passed through the notch.

"I'd say you're right. They're waiting for us."

"They're waiting for me," he said.

"They know we're together by now. That's the reason you're dangerous to them. That's why Blackie wants you dead. When you were just a boy sneaking around the ranch you weren't a threat. Now you're with me and they're worried about what I can learn from you."

"Blackie wants to kill me because I know you?"

"Look at all you've shown me about the Bar D. I already know a lot more than they think, at least I hope I do, and it will come in handy soon. You are important to me and a danger to the men on the ranch. They want to stop you from telling me anything."

"Shucks, Pecos. I already showed you most stuff, except the other way out of here."

"You mean we can get by these guards without them knowing it?"

"You bet we can. Come on." He turned Willow south and we rode on. At the rocks we headed west beside them for a while, then he turned south again and eased along a narrow path between two of them. He took a right turn then went back to the left quickly. We climbed up a pretty steep slope, took another left then back to the right and started to descend along a path that made several more switchbacks. Before I knew it the line of boulders was on our right. We were headed toward the trail I had followed here from Texas.

Soon we'd passed the notch that the two men were now guarding and then off to the right we rode by the spot where I'd found Parker and Murphy along the entrance to the Bar D Ranch. At last the lamplight from Doc Burns window signaled us he was home. We went around back and left the horses out of sight of the trail.

The doctor was standing in the open door when we

got to the top of the stairs. "Come in quickly," he urged and for good reason I was sure.

"I'm glad to see you are both still in good shape. I have to say I was worried."

"Frankly Doc, so was I. The Bar D people are on to us but I don't know how much they know of what we've been doing," I told him.

"They think you were sneaking around on the ranch a few days ago. Blackie figured you were there to kill Brantley. They looked for you all that night. They believe Andy is telling you things but they don't think he knows too much."

"I've told him a bunch, Doc," Andy jumped in, proud of what he'd done.

"And I'm sure it'll help a lot, son," he said to Andy as he gave him a pat on the back.

"That's good information for me, Doc. They're guarding the gap into Brantleyville looking for us. The truth is that Andy has been a big help. He's a remarkable young man."

"Blackie wants to shoot me," Andy told him.

"Be careful with Blackie, young man, and you, Pecos, just by showing up you've created a stir among these men. The ones with Miles Durant will follow you anywhere," Doc told me.

"Thanks Doc, that's good to know. I wonder if some of the Bar D men will change sides when the laudanum is out of their system. We need more help to face Brantley, Ringo and the bulk of the gunmen when they return."

"You may be right, I don't know. I talked to Benson about the delivery tomorrow. He had cold feet but I reassured him. Then I told him that you'd made a mistake. All the whiskey needed the magnesia solution I prepared. That convinced him we were on the level. He has all the jugs ready and will deliver them early tomorrow. All the men at the Bar D who drink will come down with diarrhea—or the runs as you call it—by early the next morning."

"And I'd say that would be all the men at the Bar D. Good job, Doc. That will help a lot."

"Don't go looking for miracles, Pecos. Some of those men can still shoot straight."

"What about the people at Brantleyville. Only two people are there who don't drink the laudanum. They might need help taking care of the rest."

"I'll do my best to stop by as soon as I can. But I plan to show up at the Bar D early the day after they take their medicine. I anticipate finding a lot of wounded men there."

"That depends on that magic potion you whipped up, Doc. I'm hoping most of these men won't put up a fight. If the worst of the gunmen went with Ringo and Brantley we'll be in luck."

"It will work, but just because a man isn't shot doesn't mean I won't have to tend him."

"Good point, Doc, I guess you'll be busy."

"The effect on a man who stops taking the quantities of laudanum these men took for as long as they did have never been studied. I don't know what will happen."

"A man can only pray for a good outcome," I told him.

"You don't have the look of a praying kind of man, Pecos."

"There are times all men find themselves asking for help from above."

"I'll do some asking myself. Good night Pecos. Take care of yourself. And Andy, you be careful, do what Pecos says. I don't want to have to treat you too." He opened the door for us.

"Everybody tells me to be careful," he mumbled. "I ain't gonna get hurt."

"I hope not, son. I'll see you both soon," he said as we headed down the stairs.

12

WELL BEFORE SUNUP ANDY AND I SADDLED UP, READY TO ride south from Miles Durant's place. Nick Farley and Parker joined us, each still wearing the same rebel hat he'd had during the war. To avoid passing Benson's store we cut across country like Andy and I had done before and rode in silence. Last night we'd gone over what had to be done. Nick was a crack shot with a rifle. He would keep Bar D riders away from us but we all knew any shots he fired could ruin our plans to take the ranch. Parker had been working there only days before. His knowledge of the layout and how things worked was fresh and uncluttered by either whiskey or opium.

Aided only by the dim light from the moon and stars we rode into the gully that would take us to the river and from there we went into the rocks on the back side of Brantley's ranch. We left our mounts in the same place Andy and I had earlier and climbed to the top just as the first hint of sunrise brightened the eastern sky.

Parker gazed down beside the rock we were atop. "The path from the river goes all the way to the ranch. I had no idea there was a back way into the place."

"That's good for us. We can get in unseen when the time comes," Nick answered him.

"Somebody left the bunkhouse," Andy said.

"It's Carney, the cook. He's getting breakfast ready," replied Parker.

"More men will be out soon," Nick said. "Here come a couple of the early rising gunmen now, Evans and Green. They're two of the meanest Brantley has. They'll guard the entrance."

Soon the gunmen rode from the barn headed to the pass on the front side of the ranch.

"They didn't eat," I noted.

"Naw," Nick went on. "The men eat in two shifts. They'll eat later."

"Only two men guard that pass?" I wondered.

"Most of the time but there are usually riders close by. One shot and ten men can be there before you can blink. Some will climb up to shooting positions that put people coming up the trail in a bad way. If we tried to get in we'd all be cut down. Brantley doesn't like visitors."

"We're coming in the front too, Nick," I told him, "but only after we disable as many men as we can while they're still in the bunkhouses."

He glared at me. "Attacking men who were asleep is

the kind of thing Ringo and his crew were good at. The rest of us considered it underhanded and beneath the dignity of the south."

"And what do you think about doing it here?" I asked him straight out.

His harsh glare gave way to a droll smile. "I'd say it serves them right."

"I'd say it will save the lives of a lot of good men, mostly ours."

"A few guys are heading to the outhouses now, Captain," Parker noted.

A loud metallic clanging arose from down below us and a man yelled, "Come and get it." Breakfast was served at the Bar D. Men raced to the cookhouse while others headed to the barn.

"Half the men eat first and the others feed the animals," Nick said. "Here come the six night riders heading to the barn now. More will go out after breakfast."

"So we need to have the ranch under our control by sunrise," I said, thinking aloud.

"If Ringo and his gang were here there would be more guards riding the ranch. A few of them might make a trip to Brantleyville or out to the saloon by Doc Burns place but that won't happen now. Everyone on the ranch needs to do their job," Nick explained.

After a while men began to head from the cook house to the barn. Some of them rode out to tend to the cattle. The men who'd fed the animals now raced in for breakfast. The four of us settled back in the rocks and waited. The wagon with the whiskey and Doc Burns concoction should be here before noon. Switching the whiskey would be the key.

We all tried to relax, except for Andy who watched the ranch with a rapt fascination. The sun was now nearly overhead when he called. "Pecos, something's coming."

I perked up at once. "Where?" I wondered.

"It looks like a wagon coming down the road from Doc's place."

After I pulled up my field glasses I scanned the road for a while, finally locking in on the wagon as it rolled through the prairie close to the Bar D. It turned off toward the pass in the rocks. "They're coming here," I told those with me.

Everyone peered out to see what would happen but the wagon was gone from sight. It had pulled into the passage that led to the Bar D and was now hidden by the rocks. I saw several men riding at top speed toward it, clearly heading to reinforce the two man crew already there.

"How did they alert the riders?" I asked Nick.

"They wave a red flag. You must have missed it with the glasses up to your face."

"No doubt, but that's good to know."

We all waited for the wagon to show up on this end of the rocks. Soon a rider headed this way at a run. Then the wagon appeared flanked by two more riders. I trained my glasses on it.

"There's an Indian driving that rig," I said.

"That's Benson's helper, Charlie Two Toes. He's an old Navajo," Nick said.

"And Doc Burns is riding beside him," I went on.

"Burns," yelled Nick. "He's really going all out."

"What axe does he have to grind in this?" I asked. "Sometimes he seems too interested."

"You'd think that with all the business Brantley brings him he'd be on the Colonel's side," Nick began, "but he doesn't feel that way. He says Brantley's behind all the broken bones and gunshot wounds he has to treat and if he were gone then maybe some homesteaders would move in here. He'd rather treat a poor farmer for a busted leg and get a chicken in payment than tend one of Brantley's hands for the same thing and get cash money from the Colonel."

"Kinda funny, ain't it," Parker piped in.

"Well, I like him," Andy added. "Doc Burns is a good guy. You can just tell."

I grinned. "I'm with you, Andy. Doc's in this to help people and that's what he does." Then I put the field glasses back to my eyes and watched as Two Toes pulled the wagon up to the adobe dugout where the whiskey and the guns were supposedly kept and hopped out. Doc climbed down a lot slower and meanwhile one of the riders dismounted near him.

Several men started unloading the whiskey. I noticed that for every crate they carried in they brought one out. While this was going on Doc yammered at the rider who stood in front of him. He got pretty excited, pounding his fist into his palm and waving his hand up and down to stress some point he was making. Then he started waving towards Brantleyville and shaking a finger in the face of the rider who'd climbed to the ground and who now shrugged helplessly at Doc. But the old man didn't give up. He wagged another finger at the guy and grabbed his own neck like he was strangling himself before waving towards Brantleyville one more time.

At last the guard threw up his hands in disgust, or maybe surrender, and pointed towards Brantleyville. Doc seemed pleased and actually shook the man's hand before he and Charlie Two Toes climbed back onto the wagon and headed toward the pass between the rocks.

I followed as far as I could with the field glasses. Then the wagon disappeared into the pass again. After a while it came out the other side and turned south. They were going to Brantleyville with a load of whiskey. Did it have Doc Burn's potion added to it instead of the laudanum the men there were used to or was it the straight rotgut whiskey the gunmen drank? No matter which one it was it would be the only whiskey around and they would drink it. The irony of it all was that whether it had Doc's potion or it didn't they would all develop the runs.

"The whiskey's here and Doc Burns deserves a medal," I said to Nick. "Now let's go."

"A rider's coming this way from the barn," he whispered.

I took a look through the binoculars. A guy in a red

shirt headed towards us on a buckskin. "Do you think he knows we're here?" I wondered.

"We'll find out soon enough," Nick said as he pulled his rifle up and took aim.

"Don't shoot unless you have too," I reminded Nick then kept the field glasses on the rider as he approached the gap in the rocks at a trot. I heard a click as Nick cocked the Sharps.

"Easy," I whispered. "One shot and they'll be on to us. Our attack won't stand a chance."

But the guy rode on, straight toward the gap in the rocks that would lead to us, and the route I planned to use to get onto the ranch without being seen. If he rode far enough in he would come close to our horses and with one nicker or whinny he'd know we were here.

"He's almost to the pass," Nick said. "I won't be able to see him soon. I have to shoot now or never. It's your call."

Nick was right, but that shot could get us all killed and certainly would cause us a change in plans. And if Nick didn't shoot and the guy found us we'd be in the same pickle. It was six of one or a half dozen of the other. We had to chance it.

"Hold your fire, Nick," I told him.

He put the rifle down just as the red shirted rider disappeared from our view. We lay on the rock and waited. My heart thumped loud enough to hear. Sweat gushed from my forehead.

The sun seemed to stop its relentless trek toward the western horizon. No one here moved. No one spoke. We waited for some sign of the redshirted rider. Would he show up behind us with a gun leveled at our backside? I had no answer. I turned to look along the way we'd gotten here. The man hadn't appeared yet. Was it too soon?

"Pecos," Andy whispered. "Cows are heading back toward the ranch on our left."

I looked where he pointed, a bit off to the south of where we'd last seen the guy in red. Next, I heard someone holler like a man driving cows and the guy in the red shirt rode out and into my sight behind those longhorns. I felt like someone had just pulled a pile of rocks off my chest.

"Let's get out of here," I said. "You're first, Andy. Go slow, be careful and be quiet."

We all made it to the horses and soon we rode across the prairie towards Miles Durant's spread. The importance of what we would do tomorrow weighed heavily on my shoulders. This was my plan. I was in charge. Whatever happened, whoever was hurt or killed, would be on my conscience. I reflected on the difference between this action and the ones I was in during the war. I was in command of a certain number of men who followed my orders, but I was under Colonel Brantley then and I acted on his orders. Whatever happened was on him. Now I bore that burden.

As we grew closer a lot of men milled about Miles Durant's barn. He'd promised to send out the word asking for help in our planned operation against Brantley. I'd warned him about giving out details and wondered how many men would have the nerve to get involved in something so dangerous, especially after they'd survived the war. But even from this far away there seemed to be many more than I'd ever imagined would show up.

When we got close enough I saw faces of men I remembered. Even though I couldn't put a name with that face just the familiarity, the conviction that I had known them before, lifted my spirits greatly. My memories were coming back to me now, if not everything at least a part.

At the barn those men rushed up to me, many yelling my name and reaching out, wanting to shake my hand. "Hello, friends," I called to them. "It's so good to see you again."

I climbed down from the sorrel and Andy grabbed the reins from me. "I'll take care of your horse, Pecos," he offered. "It looks like you'll be busy here for a while."

"Thank you, son, but as soon as you do I want you back here with me. Until this job is done I don't want you out of my sight. Do you understand me?"

He grinned in his boyish way, clearly happy. "Then I get to go with you tomorrow?"

"You're my right hand man. You get to go."

"Yeah," he hollered and hurried off with the sorrel and Willow.

The men crowded around, each one wanting to greet me. I felt honored by their attention. They called my name from every side and I began to shake their hands and speak to each and every one of them.

By the time I'd worked my way through them Andy showed up from the barn. He stood off to the side and watched, his eyes wide and a look of wonder planted on his face. The respect these men showed to me was something I was sure he'd never witnessed with the kind of men who'd been a part of his life lately.

At last I stepped back and held up my hands to quiet them. "I am overwhelmed by the wonderful reception you have just given me, my friends. We've all had a hard life for the last few years. First with the war and then the peace that left us in more hardship than a man can endure, but I'm here to say that things will change for all of us, and that change will come soon."

They cheered loud and pumped their fists high. Clearly happy with what I said.

I let them hoot for a while then held up my hands again. They quieted at once. "We're going to right a few wrongs left over from the war. You're all good men. You fought bravely under terrible conditions. You deserve more than you've gotten." I paused to let my words sink in. "This land is your home now. So, let's turn this sand and sage into a fit place to live." The anticipation on their faces was clear. They would hang on my next words like a blacksmith's vice on hot iron.

"Most of you served with me in the Thirty-ninth Texas during the war. You fought proudly and bravely but against a Union Army that grew stronger while we grew weaker. Eventually we succumbed to the inevitable. We could not defeat a much more powerful force. But many of you know that towards the end of our unfortunate defeat the commander of our Thirty-ninth Texas grew more inclined to use our fine unit for his personal gain. Many of you were treated shabbily. Others barely escaped with your lives. And some met a cruel and all to final fate at the hands of our once venerable leader, Colonel Carter Brantley."

Hoots and jeers greeted the mention of Brantley. The anger men carried against him was tremendous. We would have a motivated group tomorrow. It would hopefully help to replace our complete lack of training and organization. Still we had a collective memory of the well-honed force we once were still buried in our minds. If God willed we could use that to prevail on our next mission. The real test would be the return of Brantley, Ringo and the gunmen. They would be better organized than us and, if they managed to commandeer a cargo of Winchester repeating rifles, they would be much better armed. Still I hoped to have a few days to prepare and, if the Good Lord was willing, our plan would take Brantley's men completely by surprise.

"Today we'll organize you into units led most likely by your old sergeant and brief you on what you need to know to accomplish your mission. We hope for a minimum of bloodshed on both sides but if it comes to it let's have the other guys shed their blood before we do. We will leave here in the middle of the night and deploy well before first light. If we are successful at keeping the men at the ranch unaware of our coming we will have gone a long way to a successful mission. The future of each man here depends on our ability to remain undiscovered. I wish you the very best. May God bless every one of you. Thank you for joining us."

I turned to head over to Miles Durant's adobe. Shouts of Quinn, Quinn, Quinn roared from the men. I was truly humbled so I looked back and waved before walking on. Andy came up and walked step for step beside me, as loyal as the men of the Thirty-ninth Texas I'd just left.

After we'd gotten out of earshot he looked over to me. "A wagon is coming, Pecos. It looks like the doctor and that that guy with two toes."

"And what do you think, Andy. Is that good news or not?" I asked him.

He pursed his lips as he thought. "It's good news. It's a day for good news."

"I think you're right, but we'll soon find out." The wagon rolled up behind us just as we got to the adobe.

Miles came outside when he heard it. He nodded at me. "How did it go, Captain?"

"I'd say it went well. Unless Doc brings bad news we're on for tomorrow."

He gave a wry smile. "That will be a change. He doesn't usually bring good news."

Charlie Two Toes pulled the buckboard to a stop in the shade of a cottonwood near us. "Good morning, gentlemen," Doc called. "Charlie and I just delivered a load of new whiskey to the ranch and hauled another to Brantleyville," he said with a wink.

I took it as we should be careful what we say around Charlie. "That's good news, Doc, but you didn't come all the way out here to tell us about a delivery of whiskey did you?"

"No, if you recall I have a patient here. Charlie was good enough to give me a ride."

Miles nodded. "I'm glad you're here Doc. He seems better now He's in the bunkhouse."

"I thank you," Doc said politely then looked to Charlie Two Toes. "Will you be alright?"

"Charlie wait wagon. No want see sick paleface." He crossed his arms and stared ahead.

"I'll be back as soon as I can," Doc Burns said to Charlie as he climbed to the ground while carrying a black doctor's bag in his left hand. Then we headed to the bunkhouse.

We walked in silence until we were too far away to be heard from the wagon. "So, the lack of laudanum hit Murphy hard early that first morning, did it?" Doc asked.

Miles nodded. "He got up well before first light and limped to the latrine. Then I'm told he started moaning and when the men yelled at him to get to bed he said he couldn't sleep. Parker set up a lean-to by the outhouse, got him settled in the shed and he lay on his bedroll and shivered, sweating something awful at the same time he shook. He made a dozen trips to the privy that first morning and complained constantly of pain in his belly. He wasn't at his best by a long shot."

"Yes, that's the symptoms," Doc said. "I've read the reports but I've never seen anyone with them. It should interest you as well Quinn. You will have a ranch full of men like this soon."

Doc Burns discussed Murphy's suffering simply as a matter of fact, without a trace of his own emotion into the man's aches and pains, but those aches and pains were his stock and trade. He dealt with them day in and day out. Sometimes he won, but in the end he always lost. No matter how good he became at helping us poor creatures with the many maladies of life, there would come a time when one sickness or another would take us inevitably into the next world.

Murphy's soft moans hit my ears as soon as we entered the bunkhouse. If he was still in this much pain I wondered what he would've been like that first day. We had to take over the ranch before sunup. If men were incapacitated our job became much easier, and hopefully much safer.

Doc walked up to Murphy's cot in the otherwise empty bunkhouse and took the poor man's arm. "How do you feel, Murphy?" he asked though it seemed obvious.

"Doc, I never been like this. I'm too hot an' too cold all at once. My gut churns like a coffee grinder. Bugs crawl out of my skin. I can't stop shaking, and then I go way too much."

"They tell me you're getting better, Murphy. You'll get through this. You're a strong man."

"I don't feel strong, Doc."

"When did this all start?"

"A few days ago, in the middle of the night, I got the

runs. I hobbled to the latrine, shaking like a leaf on those crutches. Then I couldn't get back to sleep, couldn't hardly lie down."

"Have you eaten anything since then?"

"Aw, no sir, I still can't eat nothing. They do feed me a little chicken broth now an' then."

Doc put a hand to Murphy's forehead. "You're a little warm. Do your joints hurt?"

"They ache like crazy, all over."

He opened his black bag and pulled out a long, thin wooden hearing trumpet with a cone shaped ear piece and a flat base that he put to Murphy's chest and then listened in the other end. "Take a deep breath," he told Murphy.

He moved the instrument around a bit. "Take another breath," he ordered.

He put the trumpet back in his bag, patted Murphy's knee and stood. "You're as healthy as a horse, my friend. You're going to be fine in a week or so. Buck up. You can do it."

I'd waited while Doc did his work but now I had questions. "Murphy, I need to know how you felt just before dawn that first day. If you were attacked could you defend yourself?"

"I don't know, Captain. The runs hit me hard before sunup. Then the stomach cramped and my joints started to ache. That's when I couldn't lie down and everybody yelled at me. If you came at me I suppose I'd try to stop you but I doubt if I could a done it."

"Fair enough, Murphy. That's a good answer. Now don't worry, we'll take care of you."

"Thanks Captain. And thank you too Doc, but I wish I had some of Brantley's whiskey."

"That would be the worst thing you could do, son," Doc told him. "Then this whole thing would start over again tomorrow. You really don't want that do you?"

"No sir, I surely don't."

Then Doc, Miles and I stepped out of the bunkhouse and walked back towards Charlie Two Toes and the wagon Doc had come in.

"All right, Doctor," Miles began. "Will we be able to pull off our raid tomorrow?"

"If Murphy is typical of the response to stopping the laudanum then those men will not be a problem, but I understand the men who are the true gunmen didn't take the drug. They will have the runs but most of the other symptoms Murphy has will not be there. They can fight."

"I was afraid you would say that, Doc. How effective will they be," I asked.

"I'm a doctor not a palm reader. It depends on how much of the magnesia they drink. It will please you to know that I gave the straight whiskey from the ranch to the men in the hotel."

What Doc Burns said eased my mind. It wouldn't be quite so hard for them. The gunmen were our problem, not the men in Brantleyville. We walked back to the wagon where Charlie Two Toes sat rigid, the brim of his hat unbent and without the curl most men carefully worked into their headgear. Doc climbed right in and off they went. We would see him tomorrow I was sure.

Then I turned to Andy. "Tell me about the latrines at the ranch."

"Sir," he said. "What's a latrine?"

It hadn't occurred to me how much I'd been influenced by the army life I'd lived. Andy was lucky to not know what a latrine was. They would certainly be one of the foulest smelling places anyone ever had to endure. "I mean the outhouses, where men take care of their business."

"You were there this morning. They go out behind the bunkhouses."

"Yes, I saw them, but how many can go at once. How big are they?"

"Gee, Pecos, I never went inside. I don't know. They don't look very big."

"No, they don't. Do you know where Parker is?"

"He's right over there," Andy said and pointed behind me.

"Parker," I called to him. "Can you come over here?"

"Yes sir," he answered and hurried over.

"You were on the ranch only a few days ago. I want to know about the latrines."

"Well, if you mean the outhouses, Captain. They aren't anything special. There are four of them. Each holds two men. They're pretty busy in the mornings but after that not so much."

"I see, how about the bunkhouses. How big are they? How many men do they hold?"

"The one I was in, the one close to the barn, had about twenty guys in it. The other one is way bigger. It must have at least thirty guys staying there."

"Then there are thirty gunmen on the ranch. How many left with Ringo and Brantley?"

"I'd say half or more."

"That leaves fifteen or so for us to deal with," I said mostly to myself then grabbed my chin and rubbed it while I pondered what Parker had told me.

Miles walked up. "Are we going to be ready, Captain?"

"How many men do we have?" I asked.

"Counting you and the boy we have around twenty-five men, Captain."

"They outnumber us by ten or so," I said, still thinking aloud.

"Hopefully they'll all be sick, sir."

"But the gunmen won't be as sick as the cowboys. Doc says they could still fight."

"I see what you mean, Captain. What do you plan on doing about them."

"Grab Nick Farley and let's go to your place. Parker, Andy you're with me."

Once we were all assembled inside Miles's cabin I laid out what I had in mind. "We are out manned, gentlemen, but I think that more than half the men at the ranch will be disabled by the lack of laudanum, the rest are the dangerous ones. We need to deal with them first and well before sunrise. I understand fifteen gunmen stay in the bunkhouse. Six men ride night guard—"

"Two of those are gunmen, sir." Parker butted in. "The others tend the cattle."

"Good point, thank you, Parker. We will still have to account for them. Then there are two guards at the front of the ranch. If they get the runs early enough we may get lucky but otherwise they could be a problem. This is what we're going to do."

I spent the rest of the morning going over my plan. An intense discussion with a lot of interaction from the others followed. I got input from everyone, even Andy, just like I had with Parker. We all thought the plan should work and were eager to get started.

"Get as much rest as you can today," I told them. "We set out from here at midnight."

When they all left I turned to Miles. "Can you send a rider north up the trail to look for Brantley? I want warning when he's coming with those Winchesters."

"I'll send Fuller. He's got a fast mustang. But I thought Brantley would be away weeks."

"Andy heard him tell Esther a week. I think he might be back sooner."

13

Cicadas sang from the sagebrush all around. Above us an almost full moon hung high in a night sky jam-packed with stars that shone clear as we rode through the open prairie on our way to Brantley's Bar D ranch. With Andy, Nate Farley, Miles Durant and me we numbered twenty-six men who faced at least thirty-five at the ranch. But our spirits were high. I'd convinced them that the lack of laudanum and the concoction Doc Burns whipped up would give us an edge.

Now I only hoped that my words would prove true. Each man here had put his faith in me. No one made them do this. Only their inner sense of right and wrong compelled them to join this mission, the innate urge of men to step to the right side in the arena of good versus evil. I welcomed every one of them, warmed by their trust and buoyed by their hope.

We came to the gully that would lead to the river

and I stopped the troop. Ben Jeeter and Jerry Brewer rode up beside me. They'd volunteered to ride into the passage at the front of the ranch after sunrise. Both had escaped from the place a little over a year ago. Ben, while on a raid, had simply ridden off in the night, while Jerry had fled when working as a night guard. They knew all the gunmen and that might help, but I planned to send other men in from inside the ranch. Hopefully the active guards would suffer by then from Doc's potion.

"You understand what to do, don't you," I asked quietly and both men nodded. "Wait until you hear one of our men call you from inside the ranch then ride into the passage slow and careful. After that you're on your own. If no one from our team calls and their guards are still in position you must do what you think best. Good luck to both of you."

"We understand, Captain. Don't fret none. We'll get the job done," Ben said confidently.

They rode off. Earlier they'd told me how proud they were to serve a just cause again. They had once been honored to defend Texas during the war. Now each one fought to better himself.

The rest of us continued east towards the muddy Pecos River and soon entered the narrow gap in the rocks that would take us onto Brantley's Bar D Ranch. No one talked. Silence was our friend, surprise our best weapon. Everyone here knew that if we were to give away our position to any of Brantley's night riders a lot of good lives would be lost.

I stopped the column and had the men dismount and wait beside their horses in the same place where we had left our mounts before. Then Miles, Nick, Andy and I climbed to the top of the rocks so we could watch any activity at the ranch. At first all was quiet. I could see a night rider here and there but otherwise everyone seemed to be asleep.

We waited patiently. I looked for some sign of the lack of the laudanum in the men. So far everything down below seemed normal. The ranch was as calm as it should be for this time of night. When the morning star rose I felt my gut tighten. Soon the first light from the rising sun would be here. We needed to act before that. My nerves began to twitch. I had to start this attack at just the right time. Too soon and the gunmen would be ready to fight. Too late and the surprise we needed so badly could be lost.

Then Andy poked me in the side and pointed. A cowboy came from the bunkhouse heading to the latrines. He seemed in a hurry. Then a gunman raced from the other bunkhouse on a similar mission. "Let's go," I told them and everyone else scrambled down the rock.

With Andy beside me I stuck around. I needed a good vantage point to tell how our attack was progressing. The first troop, with a little over half the men, headed toward the bunkhouse nearest to the ranch house where the gunmen slept. One man peeled off at the outhouse that was still in use. The rest entered the bunkhouse from both ends.

The second group headed to the cowboy side much like the first troop had on the gunmen side. A light flared from the cowboy barracks, and then another from the gunmen's. I heard a shot from there quickly followed by two more. I focused my field glasses on it. Miles Durant stepped outside and waved. Things were under control. Two men came out, one with a rifle, and headed for the latrines. Then two more unarmed men made the run. Things were working well.

I looked back to the cowboy's set up. Men were heading in both directions always under guard from my troops. The laudanum users had no fight in them at all.

"The night riders are coming, Pecos," Andy told me and I turned the glasses on them. They were met by Miles Durant and four men who took their mounts and guns then left them to wait for latrine space. Some couldn't hold it and yanked their pants down right where they stood.

"Let's go, Andy," I told him.

"Yeah," he answered eagerly.

We scampered down the hill and rode onto the ranch towards the gunmen's barracks. As we got close I realized how powerful Doc Burns potion must have been. These fellows were in no shape to stand, much less fight. The poor cowboys would be worse off. Our plan had worked.

I found Miles Durant easily where he stood watching the scene at the latrines. "I need a good shot to go with me to the passage into this ranch."

"Take Clay Piper. He's a crack shot with that Sharps and he used to guard the entrance."

I found Clay when he came out of the bunkhouse with a gunman in long johns who rushed off to take care of business.

"Come with me, Piper,"

"Yes sir," he answered and snapped a crisp salute.

With Andy on one side and Piper on the other we started toward the passage where the last two gunmen should be guarding the way into the Bar D ranch and hopefully were feeling the effects of Doc's medicine when a man rode towards us from the ranch house.

"What the hell's going on here," the rider yelled and I knew I'd heard that voice before.

"It's Blackie," Andy let on sounding as excited as ever.

"Piper, get another man to go with you," I ordered.

"Sure thing, sir," he answered.

"Andy, stay behind me." I went on.

"You bet, Pecos."

I pulled a Navy Colt from my cross draw holster and rode toward Blackie. When I got close enough to see his beard clearly I stopped.

"What the hell is going on," he repeated to me. It was apparent he hadn't recognized either one of us in the darkness.

"The men are sick," I told him.

"Sick, what are you talking about?"

"It must have been the supper," I let on.

"Who are you? You don't belong here. Who's with you?"

"I'm Quinn. We've taken the ranch."

"What the—"

The click from the hammer cocking on my Navy Colt shut him up. "Put your hands in the air and stay where you are," I told him.

"I should've killed you that day you took Murphy out of here." He threw his hands in the air but before I could stop him he pulled down his right with a small hideout gun in it and fired.

I ducked. Hot lead whistled past my ear. I pulled the trigger on my Colt but dodging his shot had thrown off my aim. He spun his horse and raced toward the pass through the rocks to Brantleyville where I'd first met Andy. I went after him.

The sorrel was fast. I'd gotten him from a Comanche warrior who'd run up against the Yankee horse soldiers and lost. He'd been a colt then and still unbroken. But he grew to trust me and in return I now depended on him. Yet my sorrel was not gaining on the man I chased. I was in for a hard ride. Like Blackie before me I splashed across one of the streams that brought fresh water to the cattle and a number of them scattered as we raced through the herd.

He spun in his saddle and shot at me from his Navy Colt. I kept riding and held my fire. The odds of hitting a rider from a moving horse were slim at best. I'd spent one load already. I'd save the rest for when I had a better chance of putting a ball into Blackie's butt.

We thundered over the prairie, past the sage, occasional mesquite and large rocks to our left. The sorrel ran full out but we still weren't catching up to his buckskin. Then Blackie wheeled around and fired another wild shot this way. As he did his horse got tangled in the sage. He kept going, however, but I was catching up. Blackie kept looking over his shoulder. He could see it too. I would catch him well before he made it to the pass near Andy's camp.

He turned left. The buckskin slowed even more now. Blackie headed for the boulders and whatever protection they offered. If he got under cover while I was still out here in the open he could pick me off with one good rifle shot. I turned left, heading toward the rocks as well.

Blackie grabbed his rifle, jumped from the buckskin and rushed into the boulders. He climbed as fast as he could. I drew my Henry and took a shot at him, just to keep him honest, and pulled the sorrel behind another outcrop and left him there. Then I started climbing too.

A shot ricocheted off to my right, another to my left. By the look of things Blackie had a Henry too. I kept climbing. He was above me and deeper in the rocks to my left.

I moved up into a notch between two big boulders, took aim and fired at the top of a black felt hat I could see clearly. It flew away and Blackie cursed loud. I inched my way higher up the notch. At last I came to a flat opening about ten feet long and two or three wide.

If I could get across it I'd be able to scale the largest crag here. Then I'd have the high ground, and that would be a big edge in a gunfight like this.

I took a breath and dashed onto the flat. A shot rang out. Dirt sprayed up in front of me. Blackie fired again and the whine of hot lead sang by my ear. That one was close. I dived over a smaller rock and hit hard on my side. I was still exposed to Blackie's gunfire so I shook off the bump I'd taken and raced behind a larger outcrop. If I could get to the top of that big crag then I'd have the high ground. I could look down on any place Blackie tried to hide.

Unfortunately I didn't see any clear way up there.

Then I heard the boy. "Pecos," he yelled, "that way." I looked up. He stood at the top of the crag and pointed to a spot off to my left. But he was in view of Blackie who raised his rifle.

"Get down," I hollered just as Blackie fired. Andy dropped at once. I shivered. If he was hit Esther would never forgive me. I took off toward where he'd pointed and found a route to the top that he must have used to get there. I scrambled up it.

I saw him lying face down just below the peak. My heart stuck in my throat. "Andy," I called. "Are you all right?"

He looked over and grinned. "Pecos, Blackie shot at me."

I let out a long sigh. I'd forgotten about him after Blackie showed up. Then, when the gunman fired his hideout gun at me and rode off, my Comanche hunting instincts kicked in and I gave chase right off. I'd told Andy earlier that if anything happened he was to find Miles or Nick and stay with them, but Andy was stubborn and had a mind of his own.

"You should never have come after me," I chided when I got to where he lay.

"But you needed my help," he answered not rattled in the least by my upbraiding tone.

I edged past him up the crag and peeked over the top. I saw Blackie, his rifle against his shoulder and ready to fire, hunting for me down below where I'd been when I leaped over the slab. I raised my own Henry and took a deep breath.

"Give up, Blackie, it's over," I yelled then took careful aim.

He looked up, saw me and swung his Henry this way. He fired. The bullet slammed into the rock below me. I squeezed the trigger. My own Henry barked. Blackie's flew from his hands, bouncing down the rock in front of him. Then he stood, grabbed his chest and toppled after his rifle. He bounced once, rolled some and then bounced again before finally landing face first near where I'd been when Andy first yelled to me from the crag where we were now.

"You got him didn't you," Andy said in a voice only a tad louder than a whisper.

I nodded. "I need to check on him. Maybe he's still alive."

Andy rushed over and looked down. "He's awful still."

"Yeah, he took a hard fall after I hit him."

"I can let him ride Willow back to the ranch," he said so matter of fact it stunned me.

"Where is your horse?" I had to ask.

"Just around the rock," he told me as he hooked his thumb toward his back.

"You rode that horse up here?"

"Sure, if you or Blackie had looked around you'd see it was easy to do."

I shook my head. "You're full of surprises. Go get Willow. I'll see you down there."

He ran off and I scrambled down to Blackie using the same route I'd climbed up here. When I got there he was still breathing but looked bad. I flipped him on his back. He was out cold. I'd hit him in the chest near his right shoulder but the fall had left him with bloody scrapes all over. Likely he had some busted bones too. If we could get him back to the ranch maybe Doc Burns could patch him up, if he didn't give up the ghost before we got there.

I picked up his rifle and then pulled off his gun belt. I tossed them both out of his reach, just in case he came to. Then I searched his clothes until I found the hideout gun he'd shot at me with earlier. It was a big bore derringer. If he'd hit me it would have done some serious damage. I put it in my pocket.

Andy came around a rock leading Willow. Blackie was a big man but between the two of us we got him draped across the saddle. Then I picked up his guns. First I handed the rifle to the boy. "If you're going to hang around with men with guns maybe you'd better have one," I told him and his eyes grew as big as an October moon.

"Wow, thanks, Pecos. This is great. It's a real repeater."

"It sure is. You'll need to practice some but I don't want you getting into any gunfights unless you got no other choice. A gun's not the best way to solve a problem."

"You shot Blackie, didn't you? He looks pretty well solved to me," he fired back.

"Yeah, but if he dies it's on my conscience. It's a heavy load to bear. Still, he wanted it this way. He knew it was either him or me, but he thought he'd win."

"Yeah, he's almost as big a killer as Ringo."

I handed him the gun belt with the Navy Colt in the holster. Strap this on too. Blackie fired a few shots. I'll show you how to reload later. You'll need to practice with it too."

"Yeah," he gushed as excited as I'd ever seen him. Right off he wrapped the belt around his waist. "It doesn't fit. It's too big," he complained at once.

"Blackie has more meat on his bones than you. Here, let me fix it." I held the belt up to him in order to get an idea where it should go then poked a hole through the leather with my knife. When he strapped it on again it fit perfect.

"You're the best friend I ever had, Pecos," he told me flashing his brightest grin.

"Except for Esther, I hope."

He twisted his mouth up a bit, and then nodded. "Yeah, except for her."

I followed Andy and Willow out of the rocks with Blackie across the saddle like a sack of turnips. We got back to the prairie near my sorrel. I rode him up to Blackie's buckskin and checked his leg. A bunch of sage was snarled around it but it didn't seem broken. I cut it all free and led him back to Andy.

"You can ride this horse back to the ranch."

"Hey, he's a nice one," Andy said and swung into the saddle.

I headed back to the bunkhouses with Andy behind me leading Willow with Blackie still slung over the saddle. I reloaded my Henry as we rode and then kept it in my hand. I didn't know what had happened in the fight for the ranch since we went after Blackie but I took comfort that I hadn't heard any shots lately.

A rider came this way, his head down and racing like the wind. When he was near enough I recognized Nick Farley.

He reined in when he got to us. "I heard shooting and figured it was you."

"We're both fine," I said before he asked. "Is everything under control?"

He tipped his hat with a smile. "We're in great shape. Doc Burns showed up. He tells me the gunmen should feel better tomorrow. They're under guard in the bunkhouse."

"What about the laudanum drinkers?"

"They're in a bad way. Doc's with them now. Is that

Blackie?" he asked pointing to the guy over Willow's saddle.

"Yeah, he ran into a bullet then took a fierce tumble down the rocks."

"Pecos plugged him good," Andy added still excited about the gunfight.

Nick rode over and pulled up Blackie's head by his long hair. He gawked for a while before he let go. The head fell back against the saddle skirt. "Doc Burns won't do him much good. He's gone," he said in a cold, matter of fact way. "Can't say I'm sorry."

But a wave of grief washed over me. Except for Comanche who were dead set on scalping me, he was the first man I'd killed since the war. For some reason knowing he would have killed me if he could didn't seem to count for much.

"You plugged him, Pecos. You gotta get Ringo next," Andy said but any trace of his recent excitement over the gunfight had now disappeared.

"Killing a man is nothing to brag about, and needing to kill another man isn't either. I hope I don't have to go up against Ringo, or anyone else for that matter, but if it happens I'll do my damnedest to keep him from killing me."

"You make it sound so serious, Pecos." Now Andy almost sounded sad.

"It's about the most serious thing there is."

The boy didn't say anything else. Instead he stared at the body of Blackie hanging over the saddle to his horse and I wondered what must be on his mind.

"Have you ever seen a dead man before, Andy?" I asked him.

He thought for a bit. "No sir," he finally said. "A few people died in Brantleyville a while back but Esther wouldn't let me see them." He turned the buckskin around in a full circle then rode over to Willow. "Does this mean I can keep Blackie's horse and his guns?"

"They're yours, unless one of his relatives shows up to claim them. I doubt that'll happen."

"Blackie has kinfolk?"

"Most of us do."

"I suppose, 'cept for me. I don't have none."

"You have Esther. She's as close as anyone can be to you."

"Yeah," he said but his words now had a lonesome sound to them.

"Maybe we'd better let Doc Burns look at Blackie just to be sure he's gone."

"You mean he could still make it, Pecos?" A little of his enthusiasm had returned.

"Doc's the expert about things like this." I told him and we rode off.

As we neared the gunmen's bunkhouse a man raced towards us yelling for Miles Durant, his tired horse lathered up like he'd been run hard.

"Over here, Fuller," Nick Farley yelled then turned to me. "He was looking for Brantley."

The man reined up. "Brantley's coming with twenty men and a wagon. Be here by noon."

"Things must have gone well for the Colonel on his

recent errand," I pointed out. "We didn't expect him for a few more days. We need to hurry. Nick, do we have anyone with experience on a Napoleon twelve pounder?"

Fuller's hand went up. "I was an artilleryman, sir," he said.

"You're a talented man, Fuller. There are two in the barn. We need one at the end of the straightaway in the entrance passage. Take care of your horse first."

"It'll be a pleasure, Captain Quinn," he said and saluted.

14

For soldiers who hadn't been together for five years the men who'd just taken control of Brantley's Bar D Ranch were operating like a well-trained unit. Fuller had inspected the field guns and we'd just moved one up to the passage through the rocks and placed it at the end of a fifty yard long straight section towards the end. Here men were piling mesquite and sage brush in front to hide the gun as long as possible. Hopefully Brantley's men would make the turn and ride forward for a while before they realized what lurked behind the barrier.

Andy, my right hand man, had been with me the whole time. We'd left Blackie's body with Doc Burns and Andy still rode the buckskin. I'd helped him load the Henry and the Navy Colt then warned him not to use either weapon unless he had to.

Now the pressing problem was setting up our defense. If we could stop Brantley's force in the passageway we'd win the day easily. If any of his men got away we'd have problems. Canister shot from the field gun would be devastating to men in the narrow passage, much like a shotgun loaded with buckshot in a crowded hallway.

But Fuller seemed troubled. "We'll get one shot, Captain. Then the rest of Brantley's men will head back the way they came like greased lightning. And the few men we'll have shooting from the top of the passage won't be enough to stop most of them, even with Brantley's Henry rifles you got for us."

In only a few words he'd summed up what had been bothering me.

"What would you suggest, Corporeal?" I asked him.

"If we had more men we could also chase them on horseback but we really need to cut off their escape from the other end of the passage somehow," he explained.

"Exactly, Mr. Fuller, and right now I see no way to do that."

"But there is a way, Pecos. I've seen it," Andy spoke up sounding excited again.

"Captain, he's a boy," Fuller observed. "Surely he knows nothing of military matters."

"He may be young, Corporeal, but he knows his way around these rocks better than anyone else here. He's the one who told me about the back way onto the ranch we used this morning. You make sure this gun will fire when we need it. Otherwise we'll be in for a long, bitter fight."

"It'll fire, sir. This is a Yankee gun and it's almost new. It's in top shape."

"Where do you think Brantley got a such new Yankee field piece, Fuller?"

"My guess is Fort Sumner when they closed it down. I heard they sold the land to a rancher. Maybe Brantley bought them from the army, or more likely stole them."

"And the Winchesters he supposedly went after on this trip?" I wondered.

"I don't know, sir. I heard he stole them from the railroad up near Cheyenne."

"He hasn't been gone near long enough for that."

"Even when I was still here he would go on raids with Ringo and some others," Fuller told me with a sober, serious tone to his words. "They would come back happy like they'd had success but they had nothing to show for it. I'm sure that's how the Henry Rifle's from that adobe by the bunkhouses got here. I was here when they got them. Brantley went with Ringo and about twenty men, just like this time. They came back after a few days with a wagon load of rifles. I think they stole them earlier and stashed them somewhere. Then they went back for them."

"So he could've done the same thing with the Winchesters," I muttered half to myself.

"It was that kind of thing that ate at me when I was here, sir. That's one reason I left."

"And why you came back today to fight against Brantley?"

"Yes sir, and for the things he did at the end of the war."

"Did the men with the Colonel today all serve with Quantrill at one time?" I asked hoping for more of his insights. He'd done pretty darn good on the rifles.

"I can't say for sure. I don't know where they all came from. I can say that I never seen a worse gang of ne'er-do-wells anywhere else in the south."

"A lot of men here agree with you, Fuller," I told him. "I'm going to need someone on the other twelve pounder. Brantley picked this place for a reason. The ability to defend it from a larger force is important. He has two cannon, one clearly belongs here to stop men in their tracks. My guess is he has a hidden sally port at the start of this passage and my gut tells me that young Andy is about to point it out to me."

He looked at me with confusion. "You figured all that out just from me talking about how Brantley got his rifles, sir?" he asked.

"I don't know if I'm right yet, Corporeal, but you were a big help. You should remember, I served with Colonel Brantley throughout the war. I know how he thinks. Find me an artilleryman, Mr. Fuller, and have him get that twelve-pound gun in the barn moved up here as soon as possible. Every man here will ultimately be grateful."

"Yes sir, Captain, right away."

"Okay, Andy, show me the way through the rocks."

"Let's go this way," he said. We rode slow through the passage and I looked carefully at the steep sides.

There were many places where men could shoot at any attackers. Anyone trapped here would be subject to rifle fire from both flanks and a number of different directions. There were few places to hide. But we only had a handful of men to station up above.

Then we came to the open prairie at an angle almost parallel to the trail. That made this entrance hard to spot. It was only because of the buzzards circling over Murphy that I'd ridden over to look into things. That's when I saw the passage to the Bar D Ranch.

"Andy, I still don't see this other route through the rocks that you promised," I griped.

Clearly pleased with what I'd said, he had his usual self-satisfied smile plastered across his face. "It's right in front of you, Pecos, behind the bushes."

"I'll be darned," I said. We rode over and I soon realized that we could ride easily behind the shrubs on the ranch side and pass between them and the rocks. In the center was an open space large enough to hold the second field gun allowing it to fire back into the passage. Ahead we could see the edge of a sharp, thin crag that a rider could comfortably ride alongside. It led to a narrow trail that horse soldiers would have no problem navigating in single file before breaking past the sumac bushes at the beginning of the entry passage.

We could trap anyone who rode past this spot and entered the wider passage through the rocks. They would soon run head on into one of our two cannon. If they fled they would suffer deadly fire from the rock walls above the passage and those lucky enough to make it back to the start of the passage would face another burst of canister shot from the second cannon and then a charge by whatever reserve force of horsemen we could put together.

Andy and I rode back through the new passage, or as I'd called it earlier the sally port for that is exactly what it was, a path for the defending forces to leave the ranch and attack our enemy from the rear. Colonel Brantley chose the site for his Bar D Ranch well. But things had changed and instead of Brantley defending the place that task was now ours and the natural advantages fell to us, provided we had the manpower to exploit them effectively.

We headed back to the barn when across the sage we saw the second cannon pulled by six horses and headed this way towed behind its limber and caisson.

A man rode up to meet us. "Captain Quinn, I'm Corporeal Clayton. I served under you. Fuller said you need this gun up at the entry passage."

"Yes, Clayton, I remember you well. You were a fine soldier. I hope you still have some of your artillery skills in you."

"I think so, sir. They say it's like shooting a great big rifle. You never forget."

"We need the gun hidden at the start of the passage behind the sumac bush there. Make it disappear. Pile up brush if you must. You'll probably have time for only one shot so make it count."

"I always did, sir."

"That's what I want to hear, Clayton, but we need to hurry. The Colonel is on his way."

The six horses, with a man astride the lead stallion and another sitting on the limber with two more on the caisson, followed Clayton at a good trot. Andy and I brought up the rear.

As we did so Miles Durant rode up. "I heard you found a second way through the rocks, Captain. We'll need that to stop the men who live through that first canister round."

"That's the second twelve pounder heading into place now," I began. "We'll get one shot from each gun. The first one is loaded and ready to go. Once Fuller fires he can grab a horse and join our charge. We can have several men on horseback and more up in the rocks. Brantley will have to abandon the wagon. The second gun will be hidden at the front of the passage. It'll fire when Brantley's men run back from the first gun. It will get one shot as well, and then Clayton will grab a horse and join the rest of our men who'll be waiting in the passage Andy pointed out to me. How many men do we have left for that all important job, Miles?"

He shook his head, worry crowding the corners of his eyes. "If I lead that charge it will make five, Captain. Brantley will begin with at least twenty men. It will be close."

"We fought the whole war with less men and material than the Yankee's, and we won most of those fights. We can win this one."

"Only if that single shot from each field gun is effective, sir."

"Riders coming from the north." A sentry on the rocks above called out.

"That will be Brantley, sir. They'll here before soon," Miles said, wearing a sour look.

"We have enough time to do this right," I said to him. "Make sure every man knows what to do and the gun is loaded and ready to fire. Our lives are all riding on this."

"We know these guns, Captain. We used captured Yankee field guns like these till we left them behind in Texas. You can count on us, sir."

I nodded. "I trust you, Miles. Now see to your men."

15

FROM THE TOP OF A BOULDER NEAR THE PASSAGE entrance I had a good view of the second field gun that a crew now sighted for maximum effect. They would be the same men who would charge through the sally port Andy had pointed out. A dust cloud signaled the approach of Brantley's men and his wagon full of Winchesters. They were almost here. Through my binoculars I could see each man clearly. Brantley and Ringo were in the lead followed by about half the gunmen, the wagon and then the rest of the gunmen, each man with a rifle in hand.

The men we'd stationed along the rocks were all out of sight, lying on their belly wherever they could find a good spot to shoot from. Ben Jeeter, dressed in the shirt and hat from one of this morning's entry guards, would signal Brantley that everything was clear to enter the Bar D Ranch. Andy lay beside me under my orders to stay down until I told him to get up.

"Pecos, do I gotta lay on this rock like this," he complained. "I can't see nothing."

"If you can't see Brantley's men then they can't shoot you," I told him.

"They won't shoot me," he said. "I want to see what happens."

"If you do get shot then Esther will surely shoot me."

That quieted him. I watched as Brantley's men stopped on the trail across from the entrance to the ranch. Brantley rode a short way towards us with Ringo beside him. Then our man, the one dressed in the gear of one of Brantley's guards, stood and waved. Ringo waved back. The rest of the Bar D men and the wagon turned this way.

"They ain't gonna shoot—"

"Be quiet, Andy. They're coming," I hissed.

Esther had taught the boy well. He shut up at once. I only hoped he would keep it up until this battle was over. Led by Brantley with Ringo beside him, the small column rode by our second gun emplacement without a glance and headed into the passage. When the wagon and the rest of the gunmen had passed I let out the breath I'd been holding. Both men and horses rode with heads hung low. I'd seen this before. They'd been riding hard for quite a while. These were exhausted troops. I took in another deep breath and held this one as well.

"Halt," Miles Durant yelled from the passage's exit.

"You're in your own trap, Brantley. You have no escape. Surrender your men."

"Retreat," Ringo shouted. "Get out if here."

The boom of the first field gun rang out, followed at once by horrendous screams.

"Charge," Miles shouted to his horsemen and small arms fire broke out from the end of the passage. The thunder of running horses headed this way. I got to my feet and threw the Henry to my shoulder.

Andy bounced up beside me. "Get down," I yelled and pushed on the top of his head, crushing his new hat. A rider came into view and I fired the rifle, knocking the man from the saddle. More riders showed up. I kept shooting. The second field gun blasted away. More terrible screams came from down below. Horse soldiers charged past me and into the Colonel's men as our guys sallied from the route Andy had shown me. The din from the rifle fire increased.

Then I realized Andy was standing again but looking to my rear. I was about to push him back down to the rock when he called out, "Pecos, there's Colonel Brantley, he's getting away."

I followed where he pointed and it hit me with all the force of those thirty lead balls in each canister shell that had just devastated Brantley's men. "He's going after Esther," I yelled.

"We gotta stop him!" Andy cried.

"Come on," I told him, knowing he would go after Brantley no matter what I said.

We scrambled down the rock as fast as we could

and leaped on our mounts. I headed after Brantley with Andy right behind me and still riding Blackie's buckskin. I couldn't see the scalawag anymore but he'd left a clear track across the prairie. He was heading for the pass near Andy's cave. I knew he rode a tired horse. I had to catch him before he made it to Esther.

How he got past Miles Durant and his charging troopers was a mystery. Clearly he was no longer in the lead when the field gun fired. My guess was he hung back and let Ringo and his men go ahead. Maybe, after he heard the cannon fire, he retreated into the nook where I'd hid my horse the day I found Murphy hurt. Then, after Miles Durant and his men rode by, he headed out the way they'd come and found the road onto the ranch now unmanned.

After a hard ride Andy and I splashed across one of the streams that watered the Bar D, scattering cows as we did. At long last we neared the rocks that formed the boundary between this valley and the one that held Brantleyville. We leaped the creek that flowed from Andy's cave and then picked our way along the path that led across the rocks.

On the other side and far in the distance, I could see the buildings of the town shimmering in the heat of the sun. Brantley was still way ahead of me. I gave the sorrel a nudge but he already ran as fast as he could. I heard the thunder of the buckskin's hooves from behind me as Andy kept pace. The boy had spunk. I just hoped I could keep him safe.

There would likely be a gunfight with Brantley. He

would try to kill me any way he could. I had to assume he would try to kill Andy too. The boy could be a loose cannon. I'd given him guns. He could get into that fight. He was too young for it. He'd have to grow up fast.

I pushed the sorrel hard. Brantley's big Morgan was tired and much less inclined to run so hard. He'd slowed down. I was getting closer. Andy's buckskin was still behind me.

At last the hotel was in front of us and the Morgan had started to walk. I was right on his tail. I pulled out my Henry and jacked a cartridge into the chamber. "Stay back, Andy," I yelled.

The door to the hotel flew open. Paine Dodd stepped out, holding an old flintlock rifle. "You've done enough damage here, Brantley. Now it's over," he shouted, then pulled the heavy gun up to his shoulder and fired. A cloud of gray gun smoke surrounded him. The Morgan tumbled to the ground. Brantley rolled clear, a Winchester in one hand. He jumped behind his suffering horse and pumped five quick shots towards the smoke.

A woman screamed. It could only have come from Esther who must be near the hotel. Dodd stumbled out of the cloud and tumbled to the ground, blood oozing into the dust.

I jumped from my sorrel and fired in Brantley's direction as fast as I could cock the lever. He ran towards the diner. I shot again. He ducked through the open front door. I must have missed. But I sped after him, yelling over my shoulder, "Andy, go to Esther."

I heard her calling him but had no time to look. Several shots kicked up dirt by my feet. I dashed up the porch steps and dove through the open door, rolled once to my left and came up firing my Henry until the last cartridge was gone. I pulled a Colt and carefully got to my feet.

A trail of fresh blood led to the kitchen. I followed until I came to the closed door. Brantley was hurt. I had no idea how bad. I had to assume he was still dangerous and would kill me if I gave him a chance. I leaned against the wall and reloaded the Henry.

I sucked down a deep breath, kicked in the kitchen door and dropped flat on my face behind the wall. Brantley began firing at once. Shots first went through the open door then blasted through the wall over my head. When I heard the click of an empty rifle, I leaped to my feet and rushed into the room, firing the Henry as I went.

The back door stood open. Carter Brantley had fled. I dashed out after him. The sorrel had moved to the shade by the shed, but I rushed after the Colonel, following drops of his blood around the diner and up to the front. At the street I eased my back against the corner of the building and looked around. The Morgan was still on the ground, breathing heavy. Pierce Dobbs remained in the street where he fell. He wasn't moving.

My eyes followed the trail of Brantley's blood

across to the hotel. He stood in front of the porch with his arm around Esther's neck and a pistol to her head.

"Pecos," he yelled. "Drop your guns and walk over here real slow."

"I can't do that, Colonel."

"I'll kill her. You know I will."

"Then you're a dead man. If you so much as harm a hair on her head I'll carve you into little pieces while you're still alive just like a Comanche warrior would if you hurt his woman."

"You don't scare me, Pecos."

"You're already hurt, Brantley. You're bleeding bad. You don't have much time."

"It's just a scratch—"

"Don't believe him, Paul—"

"Shut up, woman." He yanked his arm tighter around her neck.

The door to the hotel stood open behind them. I hadn't seen Andy anywhere. I had to hope he was safe, but I knew him well enough to know that if he wasn't hurt he would be somewhere close to Esther right now.

A rider approached, his horse at a dead run even in the blistering heat. I didn't recognize the animal but my gut told me the man who rode him was trouble.

"Ringo" Brantley yelled. "Quinn is by the diner. Kill him."

"Not this time, Colonel," he called back, his voice as cold as ice. "I come to kill you."

"Now Ringo, use some sense. Sure we had a little set back, but it was all because Quinn showed up and started nosing around. You should've killed him when I first told you."

"My men rode right into that canister shot. Most are dead. But you hung back out of the line of fire like you knew what would happen. You set us up, Colonel. You betrayed us the same way we did your troopers along the Pecos at the end of the war."

"You know better than that. My horse was tired, that's all."

"My horse was tired too. He's dead now. The cannon shot killed him. I got lucky. You're here for the woman. I always knew you'd double cross me for her. I'll kill you for that."

"Damn you, Ringo," Brantley barked back. "You were on the run from both Union and Confederate troops alike when I changed your name, gave you the rank of sergeant and brought you and twenty of your men into the Thirty-ninth Texas. You were out of food and damn short on hope. I gave you the means to hide in plain sight. We did fine until you let Quinn live."

Before he got to the hotel Ringo got off the horse he was riding and let the reins dangle. He edged away from the building. His hands hung loose over each of the Navy Colts at his hips. "Yeah, you done all that, Brantley, but that's old news. You got a lot of men killed today. You almost got me killed. A little food and a place to hide from the Yankees don't mean squat."

"I don't know who was on my ranch, but you should blame them," Brantley yelled.

I stepped out from the diner, one eye on Ringo, my

Henry aimed at Brantley. "It was your own men, Brantley, who rose up against you," I yelled. "They did a damn good job at it. You should've treated them better. Many of those men are here right now in that hotel you're in front of. I expect they want to get even with you even more than Ringo does."

"Did you hear that, Ringo," the Colonel yelled. "These men double-crossed you."

"I don't give a damn about those whiskey sucking fools," Ringo yelled. "I'm looking at you now, hiding behind a woman's petticoats. You're a coward, Brantley." He went for a Colt.

The Colonel pushed Esther down, swung his pistol at Ringo and fired. The gunman barely cleared leather. Brantley's shot hit him square between his eyes. Ringo toppled over. Brantley pumped two more shots into him to be sure. I held my fire. I didn't want Esther to see me kill him.

But Brantley swung his gun toward me. Now I shot. Blood spattered from his shoulder. He slammed into the porch. one arm limp but still holding the Colt. Esther lay by Paine Dodd.

I cocked the Henry just as Andy burst from the hotel door, rifle in hand. "Esther," he yelled. "Are you all right?" He brushed past the Colonel, took her arm and pulled her to her feet.

"I'm fine, Andy," she said, "and I'm so glad you stayed inside until this was over."

I headed toward them. Brantley still had fight left in him. This was far from over.

The Colonel faced away from me, swaying back and forth. He held his right hand, still coiled around the Colt, to his bloody shoulder. In front of him a bearded, scruffy face appeared in the open hotel door while more peeked out from the windows.

Brantley's eyes moved from one side of the building to the other. "Look at you," he shouted to them. "Once you were fine soldiers of the South. Now you're useless drunks, swilling large amounts of opium laced whiskey and wallowing in self-pity. You lost the war. Now you've lost your minds. You don't deserve to live but I chose to keep you here. I fed you and housed you. You owe me for your very lives, but not one of you has shown even a pinch of gratitude."

A man eased from the hotel door, his face as white as Esther's dish towels, his eyes as red as a firefly's rump and his arms wrapped around his chest to keep a shaking body under control. He moved slow, like molasses on a winter night. Another followed him and still more came until the porch was lined with five half dead shells of former soldiers, hate burning in their sallow eyes.

"What a pathetic lot you are," Brantley went on. "You can barely stand, much less walk. You were once fierce fighting men. Early in the war you took it to the Yankee horse soldiers. Now you're useless and doddering old men, more dead than alive. You lost the war. Soon you will lose your lives. None of you had the stamina, the grit or the guts to whip the Yankees."

Brantley began to limp back into the street. The

first man out of the door stepped slowly to the ground followed by the rest of the men from the hotel until they formed a half-circle around Brantley with Paine Dodd, Esther and Andy to his rear.

I stopped by Dodd. He was breathing. "How are you, Paine?" I asked softly.

"Help me up, Paul," he gasped

"Are you sure? You're hit bad."

"I'm sure," he groaned. "Please, give me a hand."

I pulled him to his feet. He stood unsteadily between me and Andy.

Brantley seem absorbed by the men from the hotel who were now gradually inching closer to him looking more like ghouls from a graveyard than living beings.

"Stay back, damn you," he ordered, but the men, each taking one small step at a time, crept forward. They seemed intent on overrunning him at the pace of a snail.

"Don't come any closer," the Colonel yelled again. "I'm warning you. You're all dead to me but I can easily take away what few miserable days you have left."

His words fell on deaf ears. The men kept coming, ignoring Brantley's ugly warning.

"Stay where you are," he barked, his voice now trembling with fear. He aimed his Colt at the man in the middle, the one who'd been first out the door. "I'll kill you, Barnes."

Barnes edged closer. Brantley fired. The hammer clicked on an empty cylinder.

Paine Dodd grabbed the Henry out of Andy's hand

and cocked the lever. "I'm the man you have to deal with now, Brantley. Turn around."

The Colonel spun slowly towards us, his colt now useless. "You dumb jackass. You should have stayed down and played dead like you did along the Pecos River. Now I'll have to kill you myself. You're another one Ringo screwed up." He pulled a small revolver from his back.

"Put the gun down, Brantley. You've hurt these men enough," Dodd ordered.

"Like hell I will. I'll kill you, the boy and Pecos then take Esther and get out of here."

"You've already killed me," Dodd muttered, "but you won't kill anyone else. Esther and Andy will go with Pecos. The rest will recover from the poison you've fed them. Then they'll live free of you and your venom. Before I go I'll finish what Ringo started."

"You can't hit anybody, Dodd," Brantley answered. "That rifle barrel wobbles like a flag in the wind. You're liable to shoot one of the drunks behind me. Then I'll kill you."

"Drop the gun, Brantley. The men you betrayed are behind you. They'll tear you apart."

The Colonel stared at Paine Dodd in disbelief. Probably no man had talked to him like this since the war started. "How about I kill the boy first," he said and the gun moved.

Dodd fired. The Henry bucked. Carter Brantley's eyes opened wide. His pistol dropped to the ground.

His hands flew to his chest. He took an awkward step forward, then fell on his face.

"Nice rifle, Andy," Paine Dodd said and held it out to the boy. Andy grabbed it at once.

Then Dodd dropped to his knees, fell over onto one hand then gradually sank to the ground.

"Paine!" Esther screamed.

I knelt down beside him hoping to help. Then I looked to Esther and shook my head. "He's gone," I told her.

"Oh no, Paul," she moaned. "He lived the last five years wanting nothing more than to save us from Carter Brantley. Now he's done it but it cost him his life."

"Somehow I think he wanted it this way," I said.

"Colonel Brantley's dead and so is Ringo, aren't they, Pecos?" Andy asked.

"It looks like it, son."

Barnes, the man who'd first walked out the hotel door to confront Brantley, spit on the Colonel's corpse before he slowly turned and shuffled back inside followed by the rest of the men who'd come out with him. We watched quietly as they wobbled away.

Then Andy gave me a puzzled look. "Is anybody going to check on Ringo?"

"I'll do it," I said and headed off to where the gunman had gone down. Two riders came this way at an easy trot. "Andy," I called to him. "Make sure nothing happens to Esther?"

"Sure, Pecos, I'll guard her good," he promised.

"Don't shoot anybody unless you have too," I added.

"Don't worry. I don't want to shoot anybody."

When I got to Ringo it was clear he'd made it to the next world, whatever that meant for a man like him. I waited for the riders to get to me. As they neared I saw it was Miles Durant and Parker. The ease they rode with was a good sign.

They stopped about ten feet away. Miles pulled off his top hat and wiped the sweat from his brow. "So this is where Ringo wound up. We didn't find him or Brantley on the ranch."

"Brantley's over there," I pointed to the hotel. "He killed Ringo and shot Paine Dodd, but Dodd got the Colonel before he passed on."

"I thought you might be here," Miles said. "You wouldn't leave the ranch unless it was important. It looks like it was. Your plan worked like magic. Nobody on our side got killed. We only had two guys with flesh wounds. Just three of Brantley's gunmen survived. Doc Burns doubts they'll make it."

I let out a huge sigh of relief. The news that our men had made it through the scrap in such good shape was like manna from heaven. "That's just wonderful, Miles. I want to thank the men, they performed like a well-trained unit and after all the time that had passed since our last action that is a tribute to them and their dedication. Plus I owe a lot to my right hand man and chief scout, Andy. His knowledge of the Bar D Ranch was invaluable."

"Thanks Pecos, I'm your chief scout now. I like

that," Andy shouted and I realized I'd been talking too loud. Still his buoyant answer brought a grin in spite of what had just happened.

"We couldn't have won without you, Andy," I hollered back.

Then Parker nudged his horse up a step or two and I realized he had something to tell me. "Captain," he began seeming unsure of himself and what he was about to say. "Well sir, a lot of the men talked to me after the fight. They know how you helped me and Murphy and most figured I would be the best man to say this to you."

He started to fidget and seemed to have trouble keeping his horse still.

"Go ahead, Parker. I won't bite your head off if it isn't too bad," I said with a grin.

He got control of his mount pretty quick. "Anyhow sir, an awful lot of them would like to keep on working for you, sir and they tell me that Brantley filed for a homestead on this land after the war. He was a Confederate officer and according to the Homestead Act the Yankee's passed he wasn't eligible to do that. So he filed under Mrs. Mallory's name. The five years is coming up and the land will go to her if she wants it, and well sir, we all thought she might want you to run the ranch for her and a bunch of us would like to work for you, ah, if you'll have us."

Out of the corner of my eye I saw Andy throw his hands out. "So that's why that dirty, rotten coyote wanted to marry you so bad, Esther. You were about to own his ranch," he yelled.

Parker's news had taken me aback. I'd been so wrapped in our plans to stop Brantley I hadn't given a thought to what would come after. I hadn't been in control of my life since the war came. After that I worked for the Yankees. For near ten years I'd been following orders.

I gave Parker a hard stare. He wanted me to do this. I could see it in his eyes. Why not, I thought. I've got nothing else to do.

"Parker, I'd love to run the Bar D Ranch but that's not my job. Give me a few minutes. I'll talk to the boss lady." I headed back to Esther. She stood by Andy, her face emotionless, impassive. Maybe she was as shocked by Parker's news as I was. But Andy's face seemed just the opposite, with a grin as big as Texas covering it.

I took off my hat and held it respectfully in front of me. "Esther, ma'am, I guess you heard what Parker just said. If you're willing, I'd love to run your new ranch for you. I do have a little experience but it's been a while ago," I told her as politely as I could.

Her hard look didn't change one whit. "Mr. Quinn, the answer is no. I will not have Andy's father working as a hired hand on my ranch."

"No?" I gasped. "But how—"

"Pecos, are you my Pa?" Andy butted in and I realized I'd totally missed Esther's point.

I turned to him, his grin shinning even brighter. "I guess so, son." Then I looked back to her. She glowed like a warm fire in the hearth. "I asked the wrong question, didn't I?"

"That depends on what you really want, Paul."

"Parker, front and center," I ordered in my best military voice.

"Yes sir," he answered with a snap and double timed up to me.

"Find a preacher and bring him here. Mrs. Mallory and I are getting married."

COMANCHE HUNTER (PECOS QUINN WESTERN BOOK 2)

BY JOHN ROSE PUTNAM

When a small, battered troop of Union Cavalry arrive at his ranch with a wounded Comanche boy as prisoner, Pecos Quinn is concerned. But he strongly objects when they suggest he return the boy to the Comanche homeland on the Staked Plains as a peace offering to the new chief, Quanah Parker, in hopes of preventing another war. It soon becomes obvious, however, that someone must go and the only other man available is a raw, inept Lieutenant fresh from West Point. Fate and the Comanche have conspired to rip Pecos from his loving wife and son and send him off on a journey so dangerous that it could easily result in his all too early and much too painful demise.

Available in late 2018 from John Rose Putnam and Wolfpack Publishing

ABOUT THE AUTHOR

John came west as a young man and settled in Berkeley where he graduated from the University of California. He still lives and writes there and often gives a talk on the California gold rush to the gang at the Freight and Salvage.

He spent a lot of time digging into that gold rush too and many of his stories take place back then. John's characters are so real they'll jump right off the page and talk to you; his villains have hearts as cold as midnight and his heroes almost always do the right thing in the end.

He's working up quite a reputation for his knowledge of that era too. His blog, My Gold Rush Tales, attracted the interest of some TV folks and he appeared in a segment for the Travel Channel about Henry Meiggs, the man who built San Francisco's famous Fisherman's Wharf.

While his first novel, Hangtown Creek, a story of adventure, romance, and coming of age in the early days of the gold rush, was published in 2011, his brand new book, Into the Face of the Devil, moves between Hangtown and the sawmill where James Marshall first found gold, and pits a young man in love for the first time against a killer so evil he could pass for Satan.

Made in the USA
Middletown, DE
05 December 2018